Through the Glass

Barbara Smith

Headline Books, Inc.   Terra Alta, West Virginia

Through the Glass
by Barbara Smith

For information contact:

Publisher Page, P.O. Box 52, Terra Alta, WV 26764
Tel/Fax: 800-570-5951
www.publisherpage.com

Publisher Page is an imprint of Headline Books

ISBN: 0-929915-95-X
ISBN 13: 978-0-929915-95-1

Library of Congress Cataloging-in-Publication Data

Smith, Barbara, 1929-
  Through the glass / Barbara Smith.
    p. cm.
  ISBN-13: 978-0-929915-95-1
  ISBN-10: 0-929915-95-X
  1. Women glass artists--Fiction. 2. West Virginia--Fiction. I. Title.
  PS3569.M4827T57 2010
  813'.54--dc22
                    2009048951

Printed in the United States of America

Dedication

To all care givers, especially those related to Mountain Hospice, Inc.

Barbara Smith

Chapter 1

"I am only your neighbor, Stephanie, not your patient." Pat's voice shook. "I can handle that Jamie creep all by myself." She looked at a scrap of stained glass on the floor, a bright blue bit that wasn't worth very much, and stamped on it. It shattered under her heel, and she twisted her foot to grind the pieces on the tile floor of her studio.

"Please don't do that, Pat," Stephanie said, her hand to her lip-glossed mouth. "You're scaring me. You're an artist, not a one-woman demolition crew."

"I only wish it were Mr. Porter Jamison himself." Pat picked up a triangular piece of amber glass from her work table and threw it at the wall. It did not break. Instead it bounced back close enough to make both women duck. It landed on the floor.

"Pat!" Stephanie cried, her blue eyes wide. "You're going to hurt yourself."

"Too bad I can't throw it at that bastard," Pat said. "Too bad I can't take a wrecking ball to his head. I wish I could cut him up into little pieces and return him to the dirt God brought him out from." She stomped on the yellow glass. It, too, shattered. "Take that!" she said. She stamped her Cherokee sandal again. Then, smiling at the mess she had made, she began to sing, her alto voice deep. "Oh, it was sad. It was sad. It was sad when the great ship went down." Her voice went falsetto. "Little bitty children lost their lives…." She turned to her friend. "I can't remember the verses he taught me. Jamie and that fancy-schmancy boat of his—" She stopped in mid-sentence and scowled at her friend. "Hey, I wonder if it's still on the lake."

"What?" Stephanie asked.

"His boat, my naïve little friend." Pat's trim eyebrows rose. "I could sink his stupid ship." She pictured the small yacht, the cozy little stateroom below deck. Just minutes ago, it seemed, they had anchored in a cove on the lake. She remembered Jamie's thick gray hair, his flushed cheeks after they had kissed. She remembered the kiss, long and getting longer, warm and getting warmer. How could he have run off to Key West? Wanda? Who was Wanda? How could any frumpy, sneaky, two-timing woman love Jamie any more—or any better—than she, Patricia Yokum Tazewell, had loved him?

Rising from the stool she had been perched on, Stephanie touched Pat's arm. "Honey," she said, "let me go make you a cup of chamomile tea. That will calm you down."

"Tea, hell!" Pat said as she tugged at the waistband of her leggings. "Let's get drunk." Turning toward the kitchen, she reached to pat Stephanie's cheek, "But that's right—you can't. New mother." She laughed. "I can just see you nursing your little darling into drunkenness." She tipped her head. "I wonder if that has ever happened—Baby getting drunk from Mama's milk."

"My baby is not going to grow up with alcohol syndrome," Stephanie said. "Although if I hang around here very much, he may grow up violent. Come on, Pat. Let's get something to eat. I'll bet you haven't had any breakfast—unless it was a hundred and fifty grams of sugar that has set you off. Come on. You'll feel better."

Pat sighed and ran both hands through her tangled dark hair. "Sweetie," she said, "nothing will make me feel better short of that man dead."

Stephanie smiled her perfect-teeth smile. "Patricia Tazewell! I know you don't mean that. It's not Christian."

"Then neither am I, you judgmental fundamentalist." Pat paused at the doorway. "Wipe your feet," she said. "I don't want scratches on my hardwood floors."

"I'm not the one who stamped on the glass," Stephanie reminded her.

Pat rubbed her shoes on the stiff-bristled mat at the studio door and led the way into the kitchen. At the sink, she filled the tea kettle and set it on the stove. Then she put her knee up on the counter, pulled herself up to kneel there, and reached to the top shelf of the cupboard for a tall bottle. "We will drink green tea and get skinny. Mine will be strongly laced with rum," she said. "Jesus will understand."

"He didn't drink," Stephanie said, "—except maybe a little at wedding parties—and some suppers."

Even as Pat hopped down from her precarious perch, Celia came rushing down from upstairs, her long hair like black wings in the breeze of her hurrying. "Mother!" she cried. "I need help."

"Huh!" Patricia grunted. "What else is new?" She sat down at the table, rum in hand. "Come join us for a hearty cup of tea. Stephanie says it will calm us down."

"Mother," Celia said, her fists clenched at the sides of her gray silk suit, "you look terrible. You haven't even combed your hair. You look disgusting. I am serious."

"So am I. Dead serious." She looked over at Stephanie and giggled. "Dead-man serious, right? Thirty-nine years old and my daughter still wants an allowance. Have a seat, daughter, and cool your buns."

Celia spoke now to Stephanie. "Has she been drinking?"

"Not yet," Stephanie smiled, "but she's preparing."

"At this hour of the morning?" Celia asked as she pulled out a third chair. "When are you leaving, neighbor dear?"

"Any minute," Stephanie said as she settled in. "My husband has to leave for work, and I have to feed the baby, and I am not planning to join in your mother's libation."

"Well," Celia said, her eyes narrow, "on behalf of your children if not your husband, I find that reassuring. Neither am I." She turned to her mother. "Why are you? What's to eat? What's for breakfast?"

"Other than a cup of tea, anything you can jolly well find and jolly well fix yourself." Pat rose to take care of the whistling kettle. "Now, let's see," she said. "Where shall I begin as to why I am spiking my punch?" She poured hot water over tea bags in three cups, then carried them, one by one, to the table. "It's a long and gory story that might well remind one of Little Red Riding Hood and the Big Bad Wolf." She set Celia's cup before her. "Think of your mama as Little Red Riding Hood."

"Now, that takes a stretch of the imagination," Celia said as she lifted her cup. "If you're not the grandmother, who is?"

"Not in this version of the story," Pat grinned. "No woodsman either with a handy-dandy axe to hack up the wolf. Just poor Little Red Riding Hood and the monster."

"Who is—?" Celia asked. Still seated, she leaned to open the refrigerator, took out an orange, and began peeling it.

"My former," Pat said, "and I do mean former, red-hot supposed suitor, What's-His-Name."

Celia turned to Stephanie, who was stroking her right breast. "Who is she talking about? Are you sure she isn't drunk? What are you doing?"

"Bringing down my milk," Stephanie explained. "It makes nursing less difficult. It's better if the baby does not get frustrated trying to draw it out."

"Oh, great," Celia said as she leaned back in her chair and popped an orange section into her mouth. "She's counseling a newborn."

Stephanie lifted a hand to smooth her blond ponytail. "Speaking of which, how are you, Celia?" she asked.

"Peachy keen-o, Counselor," Celia grimaced. "I am about to depart to seek lucrative if not meaningful employment." She turned to her mother. "I got a call from the headhunters. They're looking for a witch to stir up the missionaries in somebody's kettle. I'm well qualified, don't you think?"

"Type-casting. So what's your problem?" Pat asked. "But I already know. Money."

Celia offered a one-sided smile. "Just a little loan, Mother. Just for a little while."

"For what?" Pat asked. "A broom? A black hat?" She broke again into song. *"Oh, it was sad, it was sad, it was sad when the great ship went down."*

"What great ship?" Celia asked. "Yours, I hope."

"You'd better hope not. You couldn't handle the raft," her mother pointed out. "I believe it was the Mauritania or the Lusitania or something similar." She poured a generous dose of rum into her tea. "How many greenbacks are you wanting, my parasitical daughter?"

Chewing on another piece of her orange, Celia glanced at Stephanie, then back at Pat. "Could we discuss this privately?"

Stephanie pushed her chair back. "Of course." She began to rise.

"Stay!" Pat said as she set her cup back down. "Counselors should have all the gruesome details, the whole truth, the god-gospel truth."

"Six thousand," Celia said. She looked at her cup and wrapped both hands around it. "Only six thousand for a couple of months. You don't need it."

Pat stared. Stephanie stared. Then Pat said, "You've got to be kidding."

"I need a down payment for a car," Celia offered.

"Where is this job? What happened to bank loans?"

"Get real, Mother. You know what interest rates are these days."

"No higher than mine would be, sweetheart," Pat smiled. "What's the matter with a cab? Or a bus, seeing as how this is just an interview?"

Celia's lips went tight. "Mother, it would help if you had at least a modicum of confidence in me—"

"Are you sure, Celia, that you're not putting the pot on the wrong burner?" Stephanie asked. "We've talked about your need to take responsibility—"

"Oh, for heaven's sake!" Celia exploded. "Will you please keep your damned psychologist mouth shut?"

Stephanie looked at Pat and shrugged. "What can I do?"

"You can't," Celia answered. "Go suckle your child. Unless, of course, you'd like to chip in on the loan."

Stephanie pulled herself out of the chair and smoothed the front of her slacks. "I'll just do that, thank you—the baby, not the loan." She turned to Pat. "Call me later."

As she ran her hand inside the neckband of her faded West Virginia University sweatshirt, Pat grinned at Stephanie. "Coward," she said.

"Good-bye," Celia said as Stephanie made her way to the front door, closing it firmly behind her. "Now," Celia said as she picked up the rum bottle, "about that loan."

Pat snatched the bottle back. "I may not know better, but you do. No." She set the bottle on the counter out of Celia's reach.

"You have to help me, Mama," Celia whined. She reached for her mother's hand. "Daddy would want you to."

Pat pushed her chair back and stood. "Not on your not-so-sweet life, honey pot. And don't drag your dead father into this." She took her cup to the stove, poured more water into it, and returned to the table. Colin, she thought, would definitely not give Celia more money. He would know a better way to deal with Celia.

Pat sat back down. "You already owe me, and I don't see you exactly busting your butt to get or keep a job. As of now, you have a not-so-doting-mother. I am making a declaration of maternal independence." She kicked off her sandals, and, one by one, they fell under the table. "I am already providing you with shelter and food, and there are two other albatrosses who have decided to occupy a bedroom in my house. And, just in case, I think I'd better save my resources for your absentee sister, Rosella—what's her last name?— just in case she decides to join the rest of the Tazewells in the family mansion."

Celia glanced at the doorway, then stared at her mother. "Roswell is here?"

"As of yesterday—while you were off peddling pencils or whatever you were doing all day and long into the night and with my car. Dear Roswell is present in the flesh—lock, stock, and a U-Haul full of his watercolors and stamp collection which he could sell and live on for a year and her jewelry and his beer bottle collection. Plus, in the car that was hauling the U-Haul were that ridiculous ring-maker wife of his and three cats which are in the basement and which I rather hope will claw each other to death except that they have been declawed. Can that woman wash a dish?" Pat shook her head vigorously. "Can she vacuum a rug? Not hardly. Can she flush a toilet? Well, yes, occasionally. One thing, though—she sure can turn out the junk jewelry!" She threw her arms to the sides. "They hauled in bushels of it. Bracelets and earrings, necklaces, you name it. *All day, all night, Mary Ann, down by the seaside—,*'" Pat sang. "And do you suppose she has ever offered so much as a belly button stud to her reluctantly hospitable mother-in-law? Not so much as one rhinestone. Not one phony-baloney turquoise belt buckle. She and your beloved brother are the king and queen of freeloaders." She held up three hard-worked fingers. "Last time, back in Logan, they stayed three months. That is not going to happen again."

"So where are they now?" Celia asked.

"They left early, long before you opened your gummy eyes. They're probably panhandling in a nearby alley or dancing around a campfire with a tribe of gypsies or selling their end tables. I absolutely refused to cram their furniture into this house except for one chair which Roswell had specially made for that wife—what's her name?— because she has back trouble from bending over her jewels all day, like carpel tunnel syndrome in her rear end. Ha! I am thinking that one swift kick in that overly generous portion of her overly generous anatomy would solve that particular problem, but I am not quite at that point. Inches from it and approaching rapidly." She looked hard at her daughter. "As for you—"

Celia's lips went tight again. "You don't care what happens to them, do you?"

"Honey," Pat said as she leaned close, "You're right—your little backwoods mama don't give one hot damn as long as they don't ask me to do their laundry—or lend them money. I paid my mama dues a long, long time ago. And that goes for you, too."

"So," Celia said slowly, "you don't give a damn if I go to jail either, right?"

Pat leaned back again, her head swimming not unpleasantly. "Now why in God's name would you go to jail?"

"Because I won't be able to pay my bills unless I get a job, and you won't lend me the money so that I can get a car so that I can get a job, and if I don't pay my bills, I may very well go to jail, and you will have only yourself to blame—and the bills to pay."

Pat looked hard at her daughter and drank what was left in her teacup. "Well, love, I'll be glad to come visit you. You are old enough and smart enough to pole your own barge down the river, or up. So go start paddling, my darling daughter. There ain't no more gondoliers available in this here port-in-a-storm."

Celia stared at her mother. Her frown deepened and her fists tightened on the top of the table. She took a deep breath, then stood, grabbed Pat's car keys from the hook on the wall, and, kicking one of Pat's sandals toward the dining room, she marched toward the front door.

Pat watched her. "Left-right-left-right-hip-a-jingle—left!" she called. Then Pat leaned back and closed her eyes.

How long had it been since Celia's last decent job? Five months? Six? She had been a bookkeeper at the college in Beckley, and then one day she had come home ranting about how she was going to sue the dean and the president for discrimination.

Pat had been in the kitchen hulling strawberries. "Discrimination?" She had met both of the administrators in question, and they had seemed like gentlemen if not scholars.

Celia had thrown her pocketbook on the table, knocking the dinner silverware onto the floor. "Dis-crim-i-na-tion," she had syllabled out.

"I thought that was outlawed," Pat said calmly.

"That is precisely the point, Mother! It is illegal and I am going to sue." She pounded her fist against the wall.

"Against Negroes?" Pat had asked.

"No, Mother," Celia snorted. "That is somewhat obsolete." She flopped down in a chair so hard that the window rattled, reminding Pat that she was supposed to have called the contractor. Windows should not rattle.

"What, if not Negroes?" Pat had asked.

"Sexual orientation," Celia said.

Pat had frowned, thinking that Celia was a little old for sex education and that a college business office was hardly the place for it anyhow. "What kind of orientation?" Pat asked.

She had almost dropped the bowl of strawberries when Celia said, "Homosexuality, Mother. Lesbianism."

Pat stared at her daughter, picturing her as a partner for Ellen DeGeneres, picturing her kissing another woman. "You, Celia?" she had asked.

Celia had leaned back so hard in the chair that it protested. She glared at Pat, then stood and put both hands on her hips. "I like men," she had said emphatically.

"That's what I thought. Then who?" Pat had asked.

Celia sat down again, this time in the chair that her father had always used, and it occurred to Pat that it was a good thing Colin was not present to witness this scene.

"Mother," Celia had said, "I wish to God you would wake up and smell the dung heaps."

"Well," Pat replied, "I *pray* to God that you will tell your stupid mother from Durbin, West Virginia, what you are talking about." She could feel hot anger rising.

It turned out that Celia was talking about a colleague, a clerk in the college post office. Celia had defied the administration when they fired the girl for improper behavior—whatever that may have been—and Celia had herself gotten fired.

Five months ago? Six? Pat piled Celia's orange peels into a cup, then unsteadily carried the three cups to the sink and took a deep, shaky breath. Leaning against the counter, she let it all out. "Oh, God," she said aloud. The gas tank in the car was probably near empty and Celia was probably going to get stranded, and there was a studio full of glass waiting to be made into something or other, and Roswell was hanging heavily on his mama's back again, and Celia's situation was getting worse instead of better, and who knew square one about Rosella? And of course she, Patricia-The-Tough-Love-Mama, was supposed to say "It's your problem," but it wasn't that easy, and the Jamie part was all her own fault, and who the hell cared anyhow? "Oh, God," she said again, "where did I go? What happened to that happy little Patsy person who used to live inside this skin?" Tears started. "What am I supposed to do? God! Who the hell am I supposed to be?"

Chapter 2

She was still standing there wondering which foot to put in front of the other when the phone rang. "Cursed be telemarketers and all of their progeny," she sniffled. "Two," she said. "Three. Four." Then she heard her own strange-sounding voice on the answering machine. "Tazewell Glass Artistry. Please leave your name and number. A member of our staff will return your call as soon as possible." She giggled over the exaggeration—she was the one and only staff member—but stopped when she heard the next words. "Patsy, honey, it's your buddy Jerry. Call me at—" She grabbed for the phone, knocking it to the floor.

"Don't hang up, Jerry!" She picked up the cordless receiver and shouted, "Jerry?" but the phone was dead. Then she said, "Ha!" A number still showed on the caller-ID screen. Fingers trembling, she pressed the buttons, pushed a long clump of hair away from her damp cheeks, and waited for his phone to ring.

"You okay?" he asked after hearing her croaky voice.

He was so far away. "No, Jerry buddy, I am not okay," she wailed.

"You got a problem?" he asked. "Your daughter giving you the heebies? Your snowman not ho-ho-hoing no more?"

"Oh, Jerry," she sobbed, "I'm so confused. I don't know who I am."

There was a short pause, and then he asked, "Mrs. Patsy, you sauced up already? You been into the hoochie-koochie in wild and wonderful West Virginia? It is barely daytime in also wild and wonderful you-got-to-come-see-me Colorado. What's up, Mrs. Kiddo?"

"Just tea," she said. "Tea and a tiny bit of flavoring." She giggled.

"Okay," Jerry laughed. "But I don't want you should go driving any Mack trucks for a couple hours. No bicycles neither, you hear?"

"No bicycles neither," she agreed.

"You going to be home a while?" he asked. "You better stay home, honey. I will call you back to be sure you are not riding your bicycle. You call that Jamie fella or go back to bed, okay? Your friend Jerry will call you in a couple hours, make sure you have listened to him."

Yes, Pat thought. She would go back to bed. Celia was gone, Roswell and his rhinestone cowgirl were gone, Jamie was gone. What was there to live for, even to stay awake for? She didn't even have a car that she could drive off a cliff. She hung up the phone and headed for the stairs.

That was when the doorbell rang, and she smiled in spite of herself. She brought the little white chime box from her old house and had installed it on wall of her new home. It played the first eleven notes of *Going Home*. "Go, Mr. Dvorak!" she said to the chime box, "I love your dulcet tones."

Someone was on the porch. Someone was ringing the doorbell again. "I look like hell," she murmured as she scrubbed at her face with her fist. "Patsy Tazewell," she said as she pulled again at the waistband of her leggings and tugged at the hem of her sweatshirt, "you look god-awful, but your beloved son will not give a damn."

She opened the door. It was not Roswell. It was not a UPS man. It was not a door-to-door Verizon salesperson.

"Fonzie!" she cried as she stared at her old friend, and before he could reply, she had her arms around his neck, her face on his broad chest, her tears on his soft polo shirt. He held her for a moment, then pulled back and looked at her. "Good morning, Mrs. Tazewell." He glanced at the house next door. "Do you suppose I could come in?"

Sobbing, she nodded and let him propel her into the living room. He loosened her grip so that he could put his arm around her shoulder, and, with the other hand, he closed the door. "What's going on?" he asked. "Are you okay?"

"Oh, Fonzie," she cried. "How did you know to come?" she hiccupped. "I don't know who I am."

He chuckled and said, "Well, if that's the problem, I think I can help. Can we sit down?" He tightened his grip on her shoulder and, looking around the room, moved toward the couch.

"No," she said. "I need coffee." She stumbled barefoot toward the kitchen.

15

He smiled. "I think maybe you do."

She pointed to the chair that Celia had left in the middle of the floor. "Sit down," she said. "You are too tall for me to talk to standing up. No more tea, okay?" She reached for the rum bottle on the counter. "You can have this."

"Tell you what," he said, taking the bottle from her and setting it back on the counter. "You sit. I'll make the coffee."

"That's a very good idea," Pat said, and she plopped into the chair she had intended for him. "Left cupboard," she said, and she watched as he pulled out the coffee canister and a filter, filled the Mr. Coffee with water and grounds, and pushed the switch.

"Have you had anything to eat?" he asked.

She shook her head. "Not this year."

He opened the breadbox and found a package of English muffins. "Good," he said, "I'm hungry." Pulling a muffin in half, he put the two pieces into the toaster and pushed the lever to the bottom of the slot. Holding his hand over the opening, he waited for the heat, then said, "We're in business." He came and sat opposite Pat.

"So," he said as he handed her a paper napkin from the holder in the middle of the table. "What's going on?"

Pat carefully opened the yellow napkin to full size and used it to wipe her eyes and blow her nose. She tossed that napkin toward the flowered wastebasket and reached for another. "First you tell me," she said, clearly this time, "what brought you out here to the boonies on this particular—June?—morning, Mr. Francis O'Connell."

"Impulse," he said. "I was tired of sitting around the house feeling sorry for myself. It was time to check up on Colin's little lady. I could hear my best pal loud and clear, 'Get your butt out of that chair and turn off that damned boob tube and go see my Patsy.'" Frank laughed out loud. "And you know, honey, I always did what Colin said, so here I am." His shoulders rose. "Hell, I had nothing better to do than come check on you, and from the look of things, my best buddy was right. He always was—except for stealing my girlfriend." He reached for her hand. "Now you tell me—what's going on?"

Pat frowned. "How's Nancy?"

He shrugged. "Fine, far as I know." He pointed out the window. "Ladder-backed woodpecker at your feeder," he said, but Pat ignored him. "Nancy took off a couple of weeks ago on a cruise to Bermuda," he said. "Supposed to be gone a week, but she called and left a message on the machine—she and her girlfriend decided to stay a few extra days."

"Why didn't you go?" Pat asked. "You're retired, aren't you?"

He nodded. "So to speak. But she wanted to go on her own and I had things to do."

"Like what?" Pat asked. He was still looking out the window, and she tried to visualize the woodpecker, but she was too dizzy to get up to look. "What's more important than a cruise with your wife?" Even as she asked, she thought of six reasons not to cruise with Nancy Stewart O'Connell. All six of them read "Nasty!"

Frank shrugged again, his shoulder muscles bulging. "I've been helping with a Habitat house. We finished that last week. I've been refinishing the communion furniture at church, but I finished that, too. I planted a bunch of new iris bulbs in our garden a few days ago, but I'm tired of watching for them to come up. And," he said slowly, "I got tired of thinking about Nancy and me. It was time for a change of scenery."

There was a long pause while Pat tried to figure out what not to say. Finally she raised her chin. "In other words," she suggested, "we've got the same disease. We are both babes in the lost woods. Mr. Frank O'Connell and Little Red Riding Hood. Now, there's a combination!" She sniffled, pulled her hand away from his, and used her second napkin to wipe her nose again. "Did you by any chance bring an axe? I've got a wolf that needs butchering."

"I've always wanted to go wolf-hunting." Frank got up, opened a cupboard, and found clean cups. Pat watched as he poured coffee and put the two cups on the table, then turned to retrieve the muffin and put a second one into the toaster. Butter and jelly from the refrigerator. Muffin and butter in front of Pat. A spoon and knives from the drawer. He sat back down.

As deliberately as if she were cutting a piece of glass, Pat buttered the muffin and handed Frank a half. He laid a napkin on the table in front of him and took a bite. "So tell me—where or who is the wolf?"

Before Pat could answer, the front door slammed open, and they heard a man's voice. "Mother!"

Pat dropped her muffin and put her elbows on the table, both hands to the sides of her face. "Oh, God," she said. "Brace yourself."

Roswell stomped into the room, his heavy belly jiggling above his belt. He stared at Frank, then said, "Mother, your neighbor just insulted my wife."

Pat smiled across at Frank. "Meet a wanna-be wolf. Stay tuned for more."

"Mother!" Roswell said again. "My wife simply stopped that woman as she was getting into her car and suggested that she should pay more attention to the jewelry she was wearing, and the woman insulted my wife."

"What did the woman say to your lovely wife, dear?" Pat asked. She turned to Frank and whispered, "None of us can remember his wife's name."

"She told my wife to mind her own business."

Frank chuckled, then bit his lip.

Hands on hips, Roswell turned to the visitor. "And just who the hell are you?"

"Roswell!" Pat scolded her son. "You remember Frank O'Connell. He's known you since before you were born. He was your father's best friend."

"Sorry I laughed." Frank waved a tanned hand at Roswell. "I just thought that was a piece of advice we could all use."

"Then heed it!" Roswell said, ignoring his mother. "This is none of your business."

Pat straightened and looked up at her son. "You made it his business by barging in on us."

"Well, pardon me," Roswell sneered. "I shall go comfort my wife. We will deal with that horrible woman ourselves." He marched back outside. Pat and Frank could hear angry female voices.

"That was Roswell," Frank said. "He's changed."

"A lot," Pat nodded. "And not for the better." She rose. "I don't want to deal with him or the neighbors this morning. Let's go to my studio. He won't bother us there." She picked up the two cups, and Frank reached for the coffee pot. He followed her through the living room and into the other half of the front of the house.

"Wow," he said as he looked around at three finished stained glass panels and several odd pieces lining the walls. "Is this all yours?"

Pat snorted. "Long story. Don't cut yourself on the stuff on the floor." She set the cups down and reached for a broom to sweep the shards of broken glass into a corner. "Have a seat," she said, motioning to a stool.

He pointed at one of the panels. "Yours? First, though, tell me about Roswell, what he's doing these days."

Pat pulled a second stool to face him and sat on it. "Not much. Roswell calls himself a financial advisor, but in light of the fact that he's broke, I believe he has missed his calling. He also says he is a watercolorist, but he's never sold anything that I know of." She laughed unevenly. "His wife, Marietta, —that's her name!—is a jewelry maker. Gemologist, she says. I've never asked if her parents were visiting Ohio when they made the mistake of engendering her. Is that the right word?"

Pat dropped that subject. "Celia," she said. "My three offspring," she stuttered, "Constitute three acts in the same black-comedy drama. But you know most of the story," she said. "You watched them grow up. You saw us start to get into trouble. Remember? He nodded slowly. "Where is Rosella now? Celia?"

"Celia lives here with me." She saw Frank's eyebrows rise. "Yes, I'm living at the moment with a bunch of full-grown stones in my backpack. I am, however, not going to hold my breath or my temper until one of them wins the lottery," she said as she squared her shoulders. Then she sagged again. "Only until I decide who I am and what the Good Lord expects me to do about all this." She chose a piece of pink glass from the work table next to her and held it up to the light. "I'm just beginning to realize, Friend Fonzie, that I have been fooling myself for a long time, sort of blinding myself with rose-colored glass. You know," she paused, then looked sideways at him, "I think you've had the same disease for a long time." Fortified by the alcohol, she said more. "You always tried to please everybody to the point that you always practically disappeared into the woodwork."

She looked again through the scrap of glass, then handed it to him. "And I'll bet Nancy Stewart is behind the woodwork. Bad analogy, right?"

He whistled as he set it down. "You've been reading my mind, lady."

"Welcome to the club," she said. "Colin's death. Roswell's defection. Rosella's, too. That's what erased me, but I can only guess about you, where you've been since high school." She paused. "Celia is actually a different matter which I will not get into at the moment. She'll show up later and you'll see for yourself," she said "Then you can tell me what to do." They heard the front door bang open again. Footsteps pounded up to the second floor. Then an upper door slammed. "That's my boy," Pat said. "Anger through and through. He doesn't know any other emotion or any other attitude. He's a mess—just like the rest of us."

"Not you." Frank leaned toward her. "You're a survivor."

She gave him a skeptical look, then said, "You want to know where we—I—went wrong with Roswell? You cannot possibly have forgotten about Rosella getting pregnant." Frank tipped his head and frowned as if trying to make connections. Pat reminded him, reciting the story as if she had told it a hundred times. "I stopped by the high school that morning to give Rosella the lunch she had left at home, but she hadn't been there. I decided to go on to the grocery store and then make some calls, but there she was, coming out of the bus station. She had bought a ticket for Charleston. I grabbed her and started to drag her off to school, thinking she was just playing hooky, but she started crying, and then the cat crawled out of her book bag. She was pregnant, she said."

Frank raised a finger and pointed at Pat. "That Mahoney boy."

"Right. I dragged her home and into the kitchen—I think the world would come to a screeching halt if it weren't for all that goes on in kitchens—and she told me about that boy and her. He was the Logan quarterback then, and she was a cheerleader and they thought they were king and queen of the hill, and they went back and forth to games on the bus and he always brought her home afterwards because that Mahoney boy's father—Billy, Sr.—was by that time one of the mine owners and was rich, and the boy had had his own car for years and years."

"Wasn't he eventually killed in a head-on collision?" Frank asked

"Not until after he killed Rosella with that pregnancy."

"Did he ever own up to being the father?"

"Well!" Pat said as she moved two grozing tools to the back of the table to make more space for her coffee cup. They could hear furniture being moved around upstairs, but Pat continued. "I always knew Billy, Sr., would be a bad influence, so cocky and all, and sure enough, Billy, Jr., thought he could just give Rosella some money and that would be the end of the pregnancy. He didn't even go to the bus station with her. Said he stayed at school so no one would suspect."

Frank got up and walked around the room, examining one stained glass piece and then another as they leaned against the studio wall. "Rosella did have the baby."

"I need to build some racks for those before they fall apart," she said. Then she continued her story. "I dragged her home, kicking and screaming," Pat said, "and she sat there in the kitchen as defiant as a cornered skunk, and I said just wait until your father gets home and she drank about six bottles of Coke which I told her would not be good for the baby but she said there would not be any baby."

"Oh-oh."

Pat nodded. "Colin was against the abortion idea from the start because of his being Catholic, although he had become a Baptist like me, and I couldn't very well go against his religious beliefs although I truly believed he was not right." She looked at Frank's back for confirmation, but he made no sign. "I am opposed to abortion, at least in theory," Pat assured him, "but there are situations—."

Frank was nodding, so Pat cut short her argument. "So," she said as she picked up the cup and drank the last of her coffee, "Rosella stayed in school until graduation a couple of weeks later, and then we sent her out to stay with a cousin of mine in Oregon, and that's where she had the baby. We told everyone she was working at Timberline Lodge for the summer, which was true, and that she would probably enter some college out there, which wasn't. We sent my cousin money, and the Mahoneys wanted to chip in, but we wouldn't even tell them where she was or whether she was still having the baby or anything."

Now there was the sound of angry voices, a man's and a woman's, coming from upstairs. Both Pat and Frank looked up, but then Pat shrugged, so Frank asked, "She put the baby up for adoption?"

"Neither of them wanted anything to do with it. We wouldn't have let Billy have it anyhow, not after the way he acted. God only knows what became of it. I suggested we adopt it ourselves, but Colin said that would be too hard for Rosella."

Frank came back across the room and leaned against the doorjamb. "That must have happened while Nancy and I were at the mine in Utah. So how does all that explain Roswell's attitude?"

Pat smiled. "Rosella never spoke to Colin or me again. She obviously talked to Roswell, though, and to Celia, because they both—all three—blamed me for not sticking up for Rosella and helping her get an abortion."

Frank leaned to touch Pat's knee. "That was Colin's decision."

They heard a car start. Pat stood up and walked to the window. "There goes Dolly," she said. "Roswell must have tangled with our other neighbor, Chloe. Not good. Just wait until I tell you about our neighbors, Frank. You won't believe all the stories I can tell you. Like Tiffany, for instance. She—"

"Whoa!" He moved to put his hands on her shoulders. "Finish the Rosella story first. Colin refused the abortion."

She turned to look at him. "Colin was wonderful. Rosella and I were still in the kitchen when he got home from the mine that night. I was fixing dinner because a body has to eat, especially if you're going to have a baby. I had sent Celia and Roswell outside while I talked to Rosella, but we could tell by the look on Colin's face that they had eavesdropped and told him before he came in." She smiled crookedly at Frank. "You wouldn't believe what Rosella said to him. He asked her what she had gotten herself into this time, and she said, real snippy, 'I believe it's what has gotten into me that is in question, Father.' She looked at us like she thought we were Village Idiots Number 1 and Number 2, and she said, 'I am going to have an abortion.' Colin said absolutely no, and she said positively yes, and I just stood there mashing the potatoes because what else could I do?"

"But you were in favor of the abortion," Frank reminded her from behind. Pat jumped in surprise as he began massaging her shoulders.

"You weren't there. Why did you come back, anyhow?" Pat asked as she watched the departing car. "That feels wonderful," she smiled, flexing her shoulders. "Here Rosella was smart-mouthing her father with this stuff like telling him it was just like a man to be refusing an abortion and that it was her body and she would decide what to do with it. And when Colin said yeah, she had decided to let a bum get her pregnant, she said she had enjoyed every damned minute of it and would enjoy it just as much the next time." Pat stopped for breath.

"Whoo-ee—Colin never told me any of this." Frank's hands were finding sore spots Pat hadn't known she had. "Then what?"

"Colin called the Mahoneys, and they came over, but Billy, Jr., was too busy, they said, and Colin said, 'Probably getting another girl pregnant,' and the Mahoneys acted like Colin had said, 'Probably helping an old lady cross a street.' They both just kept smiling, and Billy, Sr., kept saying, 'We'll take care of it. We'll take care of it.'"

"So you went along with Colin's decision."

"On the basis of his background, yes. Besides, this was bound to be a beautiful, healthy baby, he said, and there are always millions of couples wanting to adopt beautiful, healthy babies, and it would be better for Rosella's health, he said. He had all the arguments, even for me, although I still thought abortion was in order under these particular circumstances, and the kids knew how I felt, and they have always blamed me for not sticking to my guns. I ruined all their lives. That's what they say." She moved away from Frank and sat down heavily. Picking up the rose-colored glass, she stared at it as it lay across her palm. She frowned and repeated her question. "Why did you come back?"

"Nancy hated Utah. I never could get her interested in the Indian culture, the pictographs and petroglyphs, all that wonderful history. But she hates Pittsburgh, too. Are you still in favor of abortion?" Frank asked as he poured the last of the coffee into Pat's cup.

One set of heavy footsteps came down the stairs and went out the front door. "I hope Roswell hasn't tied her up," Pat chuckled. Then, "I wish there would never, ever, be another abortion. However," she sighed, "I can't lay all of the responsibility on those who get caught with unwanted pregnancies. Music, magazines, clothes—especially TV. Even Oprah, let alone Jerry Springer." She looked up at Frank. "You know, maybe pornography is proof of Satan's creativity."

"Now there's a thought," Frank smiled, his teeth white and even. He sat on the stool again. "But not all sex is pornography."

"And not all unwanted pregnancies should end in abortion," Pat said. "It's just that I think that kind of decision should not be made by a bunch of old men in Washington or Charleston when they won't make laws to control what brings on a lot of the unwanted pregnancies."

"Okay," Frank said as he smoothed back his gray hair. "You've convinced me."

"I'm not through," she said, but then she hesitated, frowning deeply. "Maybe I am. I can't remember what else I was going to say." She rolled her shoulders. "You're magic."

"Roswell?" Frank asked.

"Oh, yeah," Pat nodded and again sighed. "Well, after my three kids confronted me and I made the sort of speech I just made to you, the twins walked out. Rosella went to Oregon and Roswell ended up in New Mexico, right near where they were conceived when Colin and I were on vacation, and why were we ever silly enough to name them after that town? Like I said, he's a financial advisor with American Express, but he hasn't advised himself very well. That's why they're here—he says they're broke because they put everything they had into her jewelry business. Celia," Pat said, "stayed just long enough that day about Rosella to help me put away the dishes that no one had gotten around to eating from, and then she left a couple of days later—for camp or something—, and even though she came back and has lived with me ever since, she has never liked me." She closed her eyes for a moment. "Remember? Roswell and Rosella never even came for their daddy's funeral. You did." She felt tears coming again but swallowed them. "I don't know whether the two of them are even in touch with each other anymore." She opened her eyes again. "Twins should be, don't you think? Anyhow," she said, "I know neither of them has ever forgiven me." She let herself cry now.

Frank stood and turned her toward him. He put his arms around her. "So that's where Roswell's anger comes from. But you know you did the right thing."

"I don't know that at all," Pat said as she let him hold her. "I still believe Rosella should have had an abortion. She might have had regrets about that—anyone would—but it would have been better than being exiled and being treated the way my cousin treated her. Better than worrying about your missing baby all your life."

After Frank wiped her tears with his fingers he said, "That's enough about your kids, at least for the moment." She moved away. "Tell me about your glass business." He pulled a piece of Kleenex from the box on her desk and handed it to Pat. "These panels," he pointed to a glass portrait of a pixie, "are awesome."

She took a deep breath, sighed, and pushed at her messy hair. "That's my new life. What I thought would be my new life. That's all you can do, isn't it?" she asked. "Keep going or rent out a rocking chair and whine a lot and develop yourself into the saddest denial of the Christian faith that ever came across the West Virginia Turnpike."

"Church does help," Frank said.

"Oh," Pat sighed again, "I am, as they say, a woman of faith. I have faith in God and in my country and in my kids, as absentee as they may, at any given moment, choose to be. And," she said as she straightened up, "I have faith in myself as a woman and as a mother and—" she smiled, "—as a stained glass artist. That's why I bought this lot and built this house and bought new furniture and joined a health club and got rid of thirty pounds and—," she grinned at Frank, "—colored my hair. And," she finished, "I have made some good investments—real estate and pharmaceuticals, both of which have done very well because everybody has to live somewhere and everybody these days takes a pile of pills."

Frank laughed. "Sounds like you've made some good choices." He looked around the room. "I like the studio being on the front of the house. Very clever."

Pat smiled. "I wasn't sure about the glass business stuff, but I decided it might work, and it did some, but not as well as I hoped. Then Stephanie showed up." She pulled open a drawer. "See these little suncatchers? I started out taking a class at the Civic Center in Logan, and we messed around with little stars and flowers and do-dads like that." She held up a blue iris, then a mobile made of scraps of different colored glass. "Then my neighbor Stephanie came over just after they moved into their house," she gestured toward the window, "and she watched me making some of these," she held up a cardinal. "She asked if I ever did anything bigger, and I said yes, that I was working on some things, so she said she wanted a window for their bathroom." Pat reached once more into the drawer and took out a business card which she handed to Frank. Then she held up a cluster of glass pieces of different shapes and sizes. "This is one of the Christmas ornaments I've been making for the church. You know what church Christmas decorations are—everybody's discards. Stephanie and I are doing something about that for our church."

"Stephanie wanted a window for their bathroom?" Frank asked, reading the card.

"That's just what I said," Pat laughed. "'Bathroom?' Well, little did I know. I went over to their house—that one." Pat pointed out the picture window. Frank walked over for a closer look. "You can't see the bathroom from this side," Pat explained. "But I did their front door, too."

"Looks great from here. How did the bathroom turn out?"

Pat laughed again. "At first I was numb. Here they were, churchy people, and they didn't want some forest with West Virginia birds flying around or a nice sunset to go with the woods behind their house. They wanted naked people."

Frank turned to look at her. "You're kidding!"

"No joke. The space was perfect for stained glass, and that side of the bathroom overlooks some woods that nobody ever goes through, so a Riviera scene might have been okay," Pat said, "but they have a four-year-old girl. I was not about to subject Priscilla to the Riviera. So I just looked around the bathroom, and then Stephanie took me downstairs and we sat in her huge kitchen—it's at least 40' by 15'—, and we sipped her insipid coffee—she makes lousy coffee—and we looked out the back window at those woods that she can also see out of the bathroom, and I told Stephanie I would think about it. I was very busy working on Chloe's door, I said, and the side window in the Nicholas County courthouse and restoring a church window in Marlinton, which I still have not finished. I thought if I stalled long enough, Stephanie and Jack would change their minds."

"Did they?" Frank asked, looking again toward the Morrison house.

"No. I did. After Stephanie straightened me out. We got to be good friends and one day I offered to walk their dog—Daniel C. Boone because he's an explorer and 'c' for 'canine'—and she and Priscilla went along, but Stephanie didn't mention the window, so I finally had to ask right out. And you know what? They did want naked people, but not the Riviera like I thought. They wanted the Garden of Eden."

Frank looked at Pat, and she looked at him, and then they both burst out laughing.

Finally Frank pulled a handkerchief from his hip pocket, wiped his eyes, sighed, and said, "That sounds like a good idea. Let's go for a walk." He chuckled. "I want to see that window, and I want to hear more about the neighbors. They're probably already wondering who the strange man is who cuddled you on your front porch." He grinned at her. "Let's give them something more to talk about."

Chapter 3

"Let me get my key. My darling son may decide to lock us out." Pat, still barefoot, ran up to the second floor, and when she came down, she had changed to a pair of jeans and a dark green t-shirt that read "Mountain Hospice." She had brushed her chestnut hair and put on light lipstick. Around her neck was a lanyard holding two keys.

"You look better," Frank smiled. "What's with the shirt?"

"Another long story," Pat said. "Let's go. I could use a little free oxygen." She found her sandals and, as Frank opened the front door for her, she slipped them on. "These will do unless we're really going for a hike," she said. "Remember that time—"

"I remember that time and a lot of others," Frank said as if reading her mind. "No hike. Just the neighborhood," Frank suggested. "I want to see that window if you think your friend won't call the police."

"Stephanie has been up for hours—already came over to see me. She's up and dressed before it gets light," Pat said. "New baby." Pat paused at the end of the walk. "Do you want me to call her? We could go in. You could see the window the way it's supposed to be seen."

"Maybe later," Frank said. "First just outside. I want some time with you before we tackle strangers."

Pat looked up at him, his eyes a good six inches above her own. "How long can you stay?" she asked. "I have a million things to tell you—and you, me."

"How long would you like me to stay?" he asked.

"A month?" she asked. "A year?" She picked up the memory he had prompted. "Remember that time when we were kids and we hiked down to Edray and had to call someone to come get us because we had blisters up to our elbows? Who came?"

He laughed and took her arm. "Roy Nordstrom, the sheriff's deputy. Your dad was at the mine."

"And yours had died."

"And I have something I should tell you," Frank said.

"Like what?" His hand felt warm, but she pulled away. "I have a lot to tell you, too, I guess."

Frank put both hands in his pockets and let Pat lead him to the sidewalk. From behind her, he said, "I'm writing a book."

She turned, her face glowing in the sunlight. "Really! About your trips to—where was it—Nicaragua? Business? You sent me postcards, but I didn't know what you were doing."

"Belize," he said as they crossed the road to the Morrison house. "Volunteer. A couple of weeks every year for Habitat," he said. "I intend to go back next fall. They don't have many environmental health engineers down there—better known as sewer rats. That's my specialty, but that's not what I'm writing about this time."

"This time? You have other books? You never told me."

He chuckled. "Just small stuff for Habitat and some books of local history."

"Why aren't you writing about Belize? I want to go with you the next time." Pat walked up the grassy slope. "This is Stephanie's house." Behind the building, she pointed upward. "Good! The light is on in the bathroom. That's the window."

Frank drew a long breath, and his eyes widened. "Holy cow, Patricia!" he said. "Holy cow!" The window was at least six feet wide, seven feet high, the colors brilliant greens and reds and blues. "How long did that take?"

"I was lucky," she said. "The glass plant over in Paden City had sheets of what I needed, and I got the design from a picture in one of Priscilla's Sunday School books, so it went together very fast." She frowned in concentration. "Two weeks after the glass was delivered? Three? This one was easy. Stephanie helped me. The baby wasn't born yet, so she could do some of the cementing and cleaning. That's what takes the time. Priscilla, Stephanie's little girl, was really good. She just sat there on the floor of my studio and colored or played with toys. You know kids—give them a cookie and a dump truck and a paper bag or two, and they're happy."

"It's amazing," Frank said, still staring upward. "I wish Colin could see this."

They stood there for a few minutes, Pat watching his reaction and listening to the Purple Finches declaring their rights to Stephanie's backyard birdfeeder. The window looked even better as Pat saw it through Frank's eyes. She would have to ask Stephanie later to let Frank see it from inside.

Her photographs had not done it justice, but when she took the pictures to the interview at the restaurant, Jamie had hired her anyway. Jamie, a sharp contrast to Frank. Jamie was only slightly taller than Pat herself, gray-haired—both men were gray-haired—Jamie thick and solid, Frank tall and lean.

Her old friend looked down at her. "What other major projects have you done?"

She offered a tight smile. "A restaurant, mainly. The neighborhood." Her gesture included four houses in the cul-de-sac.

Frank noticed. "They're awesome. But you haven't done your own." He looked toward the Tazewell house.

"Celia hates stained glass," Pat said. "You know about doctors never taking care of themselves—and mothers going to pot—maybe after Celia moves out—"

"She's leaving?"

"Just as soon as she comes home with good news—like she's gotten a job in San Francisco or The Hague. Not London or Paris—too expensive. The Hague probably is, too. She'll want to borrow more money."

"What restaurant?" Frank asked.

Pat paused, then said, "P.J.'s Seasonings. But it never opened."

"Tell me," Frank said.

She sighed and took his arm, and they walked back down the slope and on to the road at the end of the sidewalk. "The panels in my studio? That sprite you were looking at? They're from the restaurant."

"Why didn't it open? I hope you got paid."

"Long shitty story," Pat sighed. "I'm going to sell the finished panels—which were supposed to be windows—and I'm trying to forget all about that P.J.'s Seasonings fiasco." Her mouth closed tightly. They walked on a quarter of a mile to another housing development similar in style to the one they had just left. Finally Pat withdrew her arm from his, turned to look up, and said, "Tell me about your book."

"After you tell me about your colorful neighbors," Frank said. "Who else besides Stephanie and her holy bathroom?"

They had reached a small park, and Pat led Frank to a children's sandbox. "Sit," she said. They lowered themselves to the boards that framed the sand, and Pat reached for a stick in the nearby grass. "There are five houses on Blooming Rose Court," she began.

She drew in the sand five squares, numbering them one to five. "Celia and I live in this one." She made a C in the second square from the left. "I was the first to build here. I used some of Colin's money. There were just too many memories back there in Logan, and I thought Celia needed a new environment, and—I did, too." She paused. "I guess I still do. I'm so mixed up—."

As she hesitated, Frank nodded. "I intend to make a few changes myself."

Ignoring his comment, Pat continued. "I got the contractor to sort of turn the floor plan around so that my studio could be on the front because I needed to see some activity, some people, kind of—" she smiled, "—keep track of my neighbors."

"Like Stephanie." Frank pointed to the sand.

"She lives in this one," Pat said, drawing an M in the fourth house. "She and Jack are both on their second marriages but no kids the first times. Jack is still paying alimony to his ex-wife, but that's okay because he's a dentist and makes a lot of money. They go to church about six times a week although Stephanie can't go much right now because of the baby. I've been going, too. It's my church now."

"Mmm-m-m," Frank murmured, watching her face.

"And this one," Pat said as she marked the house in the middle with an F, "belongs to Chloe and Tom Faurault—or it will if they stay together and make payments like they're supposed to. They have three children—two monster boys who you will no doubt hear and see when they get home from school this afternoon—and a baby girl who is not very healthy. She cries a lot."

Pat looked up and reached to touch Frank's arm. "Those boys!" she said. "Chloe and Tom have no clue that they come and go out of the basement after Tom and Chloe go to bed, and don't ask me where those boys go, although I will later tell you a story about them and the police and some little brown bags and what a terrible father Tom is."

"Drugs?" Frank asked.

"I'm pretty sure," she nodded as she turned back to the sandbox. "This," she said as she marked the first block on the left with a Y, "is where Tiffany and Jerry live—or lived. They split up and Jerry moved to Colorado, and nobody knows where Tiffany is, and the house has just been sold to some people who I hope will turn out to be safe and courteous drivers like most of us. That would be a nice change from the turmoil of Chloe and Tom's monster boys. Not that they drive, but you know what I mean."

"One more house," Frank reminded Pat. He pointed to the last house on the right.

"Dolly Peters. Oh," she said as she marked that block, "I must take you to see her windows. She did them absentee—or I did them and her doors from what she ordered before she ever moved in—but she says she loves them."

"She lives there alone?" He looked back toward the big houses on Blooming Rose Court.

"Not really," Pat shook her head, her hair falling over her shoulders as she leaned toward the box. "She is a very interesting woman, and we thought at first that she was married to Walker, but she's not." Pat scooted close to Frank and lowered her voice. "She's lesbian. She told us. She works for Planned Parenthood, bless her heart. People think they do abortions, but they don't. She also counsels drug addicts, and Walker is one. Recovering, of course. That's another big story complete with strange men." She stopped to grin at Frank.

"Complete with Celia and me calling the police because we thought they were burglars."

"Dolly has already told you about her sexual preferences?" Frank raised his eyebrows. "How long has she been here? It looks like the yard has just been sodded."

"She was the last one to move in—last November, I think. Yes, before Christmas. But they didn't get around to the sod until this spring."

Pat threw the stick away and reached for Frank's hand. "Let's walk some more," she said. "I didn't do my workout this morning." She smiled as she pulled him up. "I try to workout every single day, but sometimes I miss because I get so wrapped up in a project or Stephanie comes over with Priscilla and the baby or—"

"You are in great shape, kiddo," Frank said, and he patted Pat's backside. "Workout or no workout." He brushed sand off of her jeans and then his khakis. "You have yourselves a regular little Knott's Landing," he said as they moved back toward the road. "But I need to tell you about my own project. That's the second reason I came to see you," he said. "I've about decided to write a book about Colin."

"Really?" Pat stopped and looked up at him.

"He was a great guy—and had a great wife," Frank said. "But I need you to tell me more about him, show me some pictures. I could talk to Roswell and Celia, too, and maybe get in touch with Rosella."

"Good luck on that one," Pat said. She kept walking. "You really are a writer?"

"It fills my time," he said. "Which I have a lot of these days. More than I want." He laid his arm across Pat's shoulder.

"Why Colin? A biography?" she asked, moving even closer to him.

"I haven't decided. Either a biography or a novel based on his life. Depends a lot on what kind of material I can dig up and whether I can write a novel. Feels sort of like learning to be a brain surgeon in my old age. But anyhow, it provided a good excuse for me to come see my first love, see whether, after three long years, she'd remember me."

Pat felt herself blush, then said, "Spoken like a true down-on-ourselves Durbinite. Of course I remember you." She chuckled. "How could I forget my Fonzie?"

They had headed back toward the cul-de-sac, and a car was coming toward them. "That's Jack Morrison—Stephanie's husband," Pat said. "He is so good-looking—like a Marlboro man but of course he doesn't smoke. So is she. It's disgusting—good-looking and well off—he's a dentist like I said—and Stephanie is a social worker when she doesn't have a new baby, but she's not working right now except for me."

"You?" Frank asked.

"She counsels Celia when Celia lets her, and in return I give her stained glass lessons. She doesn't have any income from that, but neither do I, so we're even, and they're disgustingly good people." She waved to Jack as the car passed.

"Maybe I'll write about Blooming Rose Court instead of Colin." Frank grinned. "Where did the name come from?" He hugged Pat, and she stumbled but recovered.

"I got to choose the name because I was the first one here," she said. "I sure didn't want someone calling it Mud Gut Holler or Dead Possum Pass or Potbelly Hill like some roads I've seen in Barbour County. There was a ton of floribunda growing around here before they started digging, so I chose a kind of ironic name, kind of an inside joke."

"Tell me about the couple that split up," Frank said, "and the woman in that house." He dropped his arm from Pat's shoulder and pointed toward Dolly's.

Pat laughed and took his hand, squeezing it. "How long did you say you could stay? Do you have to go home tonight?"

He squeezed back. "Pittsburgh? No—I have a room at the Holiday Inn Express."

"Pittsburgh! I thought—" She stopped as they approached the beginning of the sidewalk. "Who ever heard of moving to Pittsburgh?"

He nodded. "We bought a town house in South Hills—Nancy's idea—and I hate it. So does she, so she travels and I do Habitat and plant flowers."

"Why Pittsburgh? Did you get my Christmas card?" Pat asked, still holding his hand.

"It was forwarded," he said. "That's how I got your new address. It's been a long year in that town house. No yard to speak of, no creek to fish in, golf course half an hour away and expensive as hell—and a lovely view from our pea-sized balcony of the South Hills mall. Charming location."

"What a crock! No wonder Nancy—" Pat began. "I guess I was just too busy moving in here with Celia and all."

"So I decided to get moving—come check up on my old girlfriend."

She let go of his hand and started along the narrow sidewalk. "Well, you're not staying at a motel. I still have an extra bedroom."

"No," he said firmly. "You have your hands—and house—full. Now, tell me, in this order: the empty house, the les—," he corrected himself, "—the single woman, the monster boys. And then we'll talk about Colin—and you."

They had reached Pat's house. "More coffee?" she asked. When he refused, she led the way around to the patio and sat down on the swing, patting the seat beside her.

He sat, pushing his feet against the flagstones to start the swing moving. "Tiffany and Jerry," she said. "They lived right there." She pointed to the red brick house next door, just beyond a stand of pine trees. "We used to cut back and forth to visit each other."

They watched three cardinals at the feeder, a male and two brown females, arguing over which one would feed at which hole. "Just like a bunch of kids," Frank said, "all wanting the same toy, the biggest piece of the pie. The juiciest sunflower seed."

"Doesn't have to be kids," Pat said. She laid her hand comfortably on Frank's arm. "No children or grandchildren, right?"

"Nancy was never interested in kids of any kind or color, but I've sort of adopted a couple of kids down in Belize." Smiling, he pulled out his wallet and showed her pictures of two thin, dark-skinned, grinning boys. "This one is Henry and this is Charlie. Ten and seven."

She took his wallet and stared at the pictures. "They're gorgeous. Do they have an older brother for Celia?"

Frank laughed and retrieved his wallet. "You—grandchildren?"

"One. Rosella's—a second one. We don't know anything about the first. The last I heard, Rosella's still working on her Ph.D. in Oriental Philosophy in Boston—Harvard." He nodded. "Her husband does something but I don't know just what. They have a boy. I've only seen him twice. He's—"she paused, "—about eight now. Styvesant, would you believe? I cringe every time I think of that boy's friends calling him Sty." Frank grunted, and Pat went on. "I've only seen Rosella's husband one other time—at the wedding. I went to see them right after the baby was born, and I went once more when Sty—see what I mean by a nickname?—was about two, but I haven't gone since. They've never invited me. I may decide to go anyhow one of these days. I'll just pop up there to Boston, and 'Surprise, surprise,' I will say, and Rosella will look at me and say, 'Do I know you?' and I will say, 'No,' and I will stay just long enough for my grandson to realize he has a grandmother on his mother's side. I don't even know whether he has a grandmother on his father's side." Pat took a deep breath. Frank waited.

"But I was supposed to be telling you about Tiffany and Jerry Yanowitz," Pat said. "They moved in," she pointed toward the backyard to their left, "about eight months ago—number 35351 Blooming Rose Court. "I do not understand," she looked at Frank, who was still watching the birds, "why our houses have to have five numbers when there are only five houses altogether. I think it would be more accurate and attractive just 1, 2, 3, 4, 5. Tiffany and Jerry would be #1, and we would be my favorite number, 2.

"Anyhow," she sighed, "this was Tiffany's first and only marriage, at least that is what she says. They were together—married, that is—for six years. No children together, even though Tiffany was young enough, and Charlie Chaplin had babies when he was in his eighties. Maybe nineties? Jerry isn't that old of course. He has two sons—"

Frank just smiled, so Pat continued. "They had two dogs, too, Jasmine and Lotus. Jerry took them with him. Anyhow," she said again, "you could tell that Tiffany and Jerry were having trouble. They never did anything together. It was always Jerry who walked the dogs. He is a very responsible person, always carrying plastic bags and cleaning up their doo-doo." She looked again at Frank. "Why can't dogs be trained to use little boxes like cats?"

Frank shook his head. "Good question. What does Jerry do?"

"Architect, he says, but not houses. He designs parks and playgrounds, things like that, although I don't understand why a park needs anything but a few picnic tables and trash cans and a gravel path or two. Maybe a tennis court and a softball diamond and a few swings and slides and sandboxes. But Jerry says parks should be planned because of the way the land lies—lays?— and where water is and all like that. He says you have to know the right place to dig a lily pond and what to leave alone for birds and bugs." She giggled. "I used to tease him about cutting down trees and digging up stumps so that new trees can be planted that won't mature for a hundred years, and the park gets crowded because somebody says you have to have a swimming pool and a bathhouse and seventy-five restrooms and eighty-five water fountains, and of course the architect's cousin or brother or nephew is just the person to do all that with his John Deere backhoe which he bought from another cousin—and there go those trees anyway."

"How did Jerry explain all that?" Frank looked over at her, then back at a nuthatch which was flying from the birdfeeder back to the woods.

"He just laughed. He doesn't have any brothers or cousins, at least not in the United States. He is from Belgrade, or his father was. His real name is Jerzy, but his family moved to Sicily when he was little, and then they changed their name so that it wouldn't be all consonants with no vowels. They decided to call him Jerry, but Yanowitz isn't much of an improvement, is it. Jerry," she said as she brushed a mosquito from Frank's arm, "was born when his mother was sixteen. His father got his mother pregnant when she was fifteen and he was forty-three. Jerry says they got married because otherwise her parents would have probably killed him. That's the way they did things in the old country, he says." She paused for breath. "I wish— well, I'm just glad he was able to sell the house so fast. And he likes Colorado."

"Everybody does," Frank said.

They could hear the Faurault baby crying, and Pat looked in that direction but did not comment. Deafening music began from the same direction, and then loud, young voices shouted back and forth. "I told you," Pat said. "That's those delinquent boys. Why aren't they in school? Maybe they've been expelled. "

"You like Jerry a lot," Frank noted.

Pat straightened her shoulders. "He is a great friend," she said. "And so funny. And he always seemed to know just when I needed a little company because Celia is so difficult and all. And I'm doing all the talking. Tell me—" she began.

"You spent a lot of time together?" Frank was watching her closely.

"Not really. The first time I really spoke to Jerry except to wave sometimes and take their dinner when they were moving in was when Celia and I were out for a walk one night. She was ahead of me in those hot pink shorts of hers, which I find rather embarrassing although Celia has a very nice figure. Anyhow, here came Jerry's truck, and he stopped and said hello and I said hello and he hopped right out of that truck and said, in his funny little accent, 'You use company? I walk with you.' And he did. Celia was very surprised because she thinks her mother is too old for such goings-on, even if the man is just a friendly neighbor."

"You're definitely not," Frank said. He put his hand on top of hers as it lay on his arm. "Definitely not."

They sat quietly on the swing, listening to birds and the baby and the blast of acid rock. Then Pat said, "Jerry's mother lived here in West Virginia all of her adult life—after they came from Italy— Jerry's father was a miner—but she never spoke more than a few words of English, probably just enough to ask for milk at the grocery store. His father died, and then she had to raise Jerry and seven other children. She always took the little ones with her when she cleaned houses for the rich people around Clarksburg, where Jerry says they were living. Jerry says she crocheted afghans and doilies and that kind of thing, which she sold to neighbors and took to church bazaars and street fairs." She frowned. "He said church bazaars, I'm sure, but things at church bazaars are usually donated, although I don't give away my glass pieces except maybe a few wind chimes and suncatchers for good causes now and again."

Frank stroked her hand.

"I can make those," Pat explained, "from throwaway scraps and bits of wire. Nobody knows the glass was not cut especially."

"Speaking of which—are you okay financially?" Frank asked.

"We're fine," Pat said. "Doing very well, thank you. I talked Colin into buying some real estate because my daddy always said that after everything else passes away, there will still be land, and I decided pharmaceuticals because—," she laughed, "—all my friends started taking hormones and now everybody in the world is taking pills —except me."

"And me," he smiled. "Just let me know if you ever need help." She leaned against him. "Tiffany and Jerry," he said as he pulled her close.

"Tiffany told me," Pat said, "that Jerry told her that sometimes Jerry's mother would set up a table and sell things along the road where they lived in Norton after they were evicted from their house in Brownton, which is where they lived after Clarksburg. They never could pay their rent."

"What did Jerry's father die of?" Frank asked. "Emphysema, I'll bet."

Pat nodded. "It's always emphysema or an accident, isn't it. Jerry says that's why the big companies offer good benefits. The miners don't live long enough to collect." She sighed, then brightened. "You should have heard Tiffany imitate Jerry. It was funny, but she was always being sarcastic so it wasn't really funny. 'Jerry's mama, she bake bread. Can peaches. Hem towels,' Tiffany would say. 'Find shiny stones. Sell twigs. She sell everything but kids,' Tiffany would say. 'My Jerry swear he never miner. Deliver papers. Cut grass. Sweep back porches. Shine shoes. Shovel snow, he say. All like that,' Tiffany would say. 'Jerry work, work, work. No play. No fun. Work, work, work.'"

"How did he get to be an architect?" Frank asked as he eased Pat to an upright position, then got up from the swing and walked to the edge of the patio. He leaned to pull a weed from the edge of the flagstones.

"One of the high muckety-mucks in the mine office sort of sponsored him," Pat said, "and Jerry ended up being able to go to college because that man helped him. Jerry really is a very hard worker and a good friend." She was remembering the bottles of homemade wine they had shared right there on her patio, the warmth of his arm around her when she was feeling bad, his wise and funny words about Celia, about Chloe and Tom, and especially about Tiffany. Frank was right. In the seven months before Jerry left, they actually had spent a lot of time together.

"What about Tiffany?" Frank asked, reading Pat's mind. "What did she do? Work?"

"Ha!" Pat exploded. "Now there's a story—a book—for you." Pat pushed with her feet and set the swing in motion again. Frank reached down and pulled another small weed. "She says she is African-American," Pat said, "but I think she is really Mexican. She probably changes her story depending upon what's popular at the time."

Frank turned to look at Pat and smiled. "You don't like Tiffany."

"At first she was okay. She says her family is from Michigan, but I detected some kind of accent, and it did not exactly come from Detroit. I'm not sure her name is really Tiffany either. Maybe it's Juanita or Maria Teresa and she changed it."

"Does she work?"

"Not in your terms." Pat shifted to a more comfortable position. "I asked her about that the very first time she came over, and she said she worked professionally before they moved to Blooming Rose, but I was suspicious. It sounded funny, and she said there were very few jobs in her field around Logan. I asked Chloe about it one time because I thought they were getting to be friends, but Chloe is so preoccupied with those boys and that little baby that she doesn't even know what day it is. She acted like she didn't know what I was talking about." Pat said. "I suspect she did, though."

Frank's eyebrows rose.

Pat continued, the swing creaking with her movements. "Chloe came over one day, and there I was in my studio, still wearing the t-shirt I had been sleeping in. They're much more comfortable than those slinky, skimpy things that men buy for women to be sexy and then women think they have to wear them even though they are cruelly uncomfortable and the women don't want to be sexy anyhow." She did not wait for an answer. "My t-shirt says 'Walk for Life' and Jerry gave it to me because it was too small for him and Tiffany did not want anything to do with cancer. I promised to walk next year. I hate to beg people to sponsor me, though, so I'll probably just make a contribution. That should count, don't you think?"

Frank smiled and nodded at the birds. "Absolutely," he said.

"Oh—well, she showed up at my front door at eight o'clock that day. Thank God I had pulled on some leggings—and so on—, and here came Tiffany, smiling like Dorothy Lamour, her hips moving like she was doing a rumba with Bob Hope—remember that?—and all dressed up in a red and yellow flounced skirt and a white off-the-shoulder blouse like Carmen Miranda, and I wanted to be friends with her, so I said she looked like she was ready to lead a funeral parade. I really meant just 'parade.'"

Frank laughed out loud. "She must have loved that."

"That was a mistake," Pat admitted. "She said, 'I am from Detroit, Mrs. Tazewell, not New Orleans,' but I can be clever even if I'm not always politically correct, so I said, smooth as yogurt, 'I wasn't thinking of New Orleans. New York,' I said. 'Did I say *funeral*? I meant Easter.'"

"I'll bet that wasn't the end of it." Frank grinned. The music had stopped momentarily, but now it started again.

Pat got up off the swing and imitated Tiffany's swagger and frosty speech. "'I do not do parades,' she said. 'Not today or any day.' So I changed the subject as fast as I could and asked how their house was coming along. She smiled, and I remember the breeze came up, and she smoothed back her gorgeous long black hair—which is straight like Hispanic, not kinky like African-American or too curly like mine—, and she said they were not ready for company yet but she would like me to do something special for their front door if I was a stained glass lady like Stephanie told her. And that is the reason all the neighborhood has stained glass doors and windows and why those bratty boys call me the old stained glass woman. Stephanie's bathroom and Tiffany's front door and then everybody."

"Not yours," Frank observed again.

"Not yet."

Frank followed her as they moved toward the door. "How do you decide on a design?" he asked.

"I ask a lot of questions and they make a lot of suggestions. You have to know a lot about people before you can design their lives." She turned to smile at him. "That's how I like to think about my work—designing people's lives. After all, if you're going to be coming and going through the same door a dozen times a day, that door is going to have an enormous influence on your attitude. Just imagine coming or going three or four times a day through a door with gargoyles or druids or vampires on it." She swung her arms in a wide gesture. "Then imagine limpid pools and water lilies and a gray and white crane. A good door is better than aromatherapy, although I approve of that, too. So does Jerry. He brought me a bottle of orange and ginger hand lotion once, and it really did stimulate my right brain, you might say."

"You do like Jerry," Frank observed.

"He's a lot like you," she said as she led the way through the kitchen. "Maybe a combination of you and Colin and my mother. Your steadiness and good sense, Colin's being an immigrant and a hard worker and handsome—not that you're not," she smiled, "and my mother's sense of humor. He is so funny!"

Frank looked at his watch. "You still haven't had anything much to eat, Patsy, and I'm getting hungry myself."

"Oh, my gosh!" Pat's hand went to her head. "I am so stupid! Of course you are. I'll just—"

"No," Frank said. "We're going to a diner I saw on my way here. A couple of miles? I dig diners."

She frowned. "That reminds me. You got my address from my Christmas card?"

He stood and adjusted his belt. "You're also in the phone book. I called."

"You did?" she asked. She moved to the sink and began rinsing coffee cups.

"Last Thursday. Roswell said you were at church. He told me how to get here. He didn't tell you." Frank reached for a towel.

Lips tight, she shook her head. "Dishwasher." She opened it and set the cups inside. "No, Roswell did not tell me."

Frank grinned. "I thought maybe that was why you were drinking this morning —in anticipation of my visit."

Pat giggled, then reached high to touch Frank's cheek. "Not quite, although if your coming had been the reason, I would have been celebrating. I am very, very glad to see you."

"Then why the liquor?" he asked.

She frowned and bit her lip. "I'll tell you. In fact, I'll show you. We'll be going close to that damned P. J.'s Seasonings. I'll tell you the rest about Tiffany and Jerry on the way, too. You won't believe any of it." She closed the dishwasher, turned off the water in the sink, and moved toward the stairs. "Find a book or something. I'll be right down," she said. "And you have to tell me about Nancy."

Chapter 4

The upstairs bathroom was a royal mess. It was a good thing, Pat decided, that she had directed Frank to the half-bath near her studio. She looked at the discarded towels, Celia's pajamas hanging over the shower curtain rod, the rings of scum on the sink. Not able to resist, Pat picked up a towel and wiped out the sink. Then she sopped up the water on the floor. She threw the towels and Celia's clothes into the hamper, imagining an equally disgusting situation in the guest bathroom which Roswell and Marietta had been using. No, Pat thought, she would not clean it up, at least not now.

She turned to the mirror, shocked by what she saw. This old woman, her neck crepey, her eyes dark-circled, her hair in need of serious help—could not possibly be the wife of that handsome young Colin Tazewell. This was not the high school cheerleader and cross-country runner who had dated Francis O'Connell and had nicknamed him "Fonzie." Who, dear God, was this old hag?

Pat opened the bathroom door, went to the head of the stairs, and called, "Frank?"

He answered, and she said, "Fifteen minutes?"

In twenty minutes she had showered, shampooed and dried her hair, creamed her face and neck, applied make-up, and put on tight new jeans and a red blazer. This sixty-two-year-old might no longer be Patsy Yokum Tazewell, but at least she was a presentable Patricia Tazewell, Artist in Stained Glass.

"Wow!" Frank said as she rejoined him.

She smiled and reached for his outstretched hand. "Imagine what another fifteen minutes might have done."

He squeezed her hand. "I'm satisfied," he said. "What's your perfume?"

"Estee Lauder. Pleasure," she said.

"You are indeed."

As they pulled away from the curb, Pat pointed to the Faurault house. "Hear the baby still crying? It drives me nuts, wondering if that poor child is all right."

He shook his head. "I didn't notice. I found the paper and was reading about the economic situation in California."

Pat groaned. "And they talk about poor old West Virginia."

"Finish telling me," he reminded her. "What happened to Jerry?"

A mail truck went by, and the woman driving it waved, her thumb raised high. Pat grinned at her, then said to Frank, "I told you Tiffany and Jerry had no children of their own, but Jerry has two sons— teenagers. I talked to them for only a few minutes, but they seemed hugely different from Chloe and Tom's kids." She gestured to indicate the direction Frank should take.

"Anyhow," she continued, "they came to visit their dad—they've been living with their mother in Colorado," she said. "Jerry has visited them out there, and they taught him to ski. Their mother and Jerry are still good friends, but she has remarried, a man who owns one of the restaurants in Steamboat Springs." Pat pointed directions again. "Jerry says there are a million great restaurants, more restaurants than residents because it is a tourist town. Anyhow," she said, "Jake and Junior—I suppose his name is Jerry, too—came to spend last Christmas with Tiffany and Jerry soon after they moved here. Jerry was busy designing a golf course or something, so he gave the boys his truck and they decided to cruise around. They saw Tiffany's car at the Starlight Motel and decided to stop by because she had said she was the receptionist. But Tiffany was not at the desk, and the man who was there thought the boys were interested in a particular kind of service which is frequently associated with motels. That ignorant man said he had only one girl available that afternoon—a girl named Tiffany—but if they wanted to, they could wait until she finished with her current customer.

"Needless to say," Pat said as she enjoyed the look on Frank's face, "that blew her cover." She giggled. "Literally as well as figuratively. The boys said no thank you and rushed back and told Jerry. They had never liked Tiffany very well anyhow, Jerry says, and now he didn't either. So he left the boys standing on the road in

the park, wondering how they would get back to Jerry's house, and
Jerry grabbed his truck and wheeled himself straight out to that motel.
He confronted Tiffany, and then he went back and picked up the
boys and took them home, and the three of them threw Tiffany's
clothes and knick-knacks and all her stuff right into the street." She
laughed. "I was glad I didn't have to go anywhere because I couldn't
have gotten around the stacks of trash. And it's a good thing their
front door is sturdy. Jerry slammed it like a time bomb when he and
the boys left." She looked at Frank. "Why is it that men are door-
slammers? It must provide a power surge or something."

"The end of another not-so-beautiful romance," Frank suggested
as he drove up the ramp and onto the interstate.

"Another?" Pat asked.

Frank ignored her question. "So Jerry left."

"He came over while the boys were packing up and said good-
bye and said that he hoped to become a ski instructor for seniors and
that he would teach me when I came out to see them." She felt her
face redden, remembering Jerry's farewell kiss. "Jerry said he would
be getting a divorce."

"He calls?" Frank asked.

She nodded, then frowned. "This morning, before you came.
He said he would call back in a few hours, but he didn't."

"He will," Frank promised.

"Tiffany wanted me to make her a stained glass monkey for
their kitchen window." Pat chuckled.

"Did you?"

"I have never in my life even drawn a monkey," Pat said, "let
alone made one into stained glass. Jerry said he didn't want me to,
and he told Tiffany, 'I don't pay for no monkeys,' and he told me he
was opposed to all monkeys because 'buggy,' he said, and Tiffany
said she would pay for it herself, and he asked her with what, and she
said 'You watch me, big boy,' and he said, 'No more like that or you
gonna fancy-dancy yourself out your fancy-dancy front door.' So I
didn't even think about doing monkeys."

"Good," Frank nodded. "Tell me about the other neighbors."

"Later. Turn right at the next exit," Pat suggested.

He let a lumber truck pass, then took the ramp. She pointed to a parking lot coming up on their left. Frank waited for a car coming from the other direction and then pulled onto the new black asphalt. In front of them a limestone building glowed cleanly in the sunlight. Huge brown plastic letters bolted to the stone blocks read "P. J.'s Seasonings." The windows and the door had been covered with plywood. Lush maples trees were coming into full leaf beyond the building, and tulips had recently dropped their petals along the walkway. Frank watched as a score of pigeons, startled by the appearance of the car, settled back along the rain gutters. Hammering sounded from the rear of the building, some kind of construction going on. Pat frowned with curiosity.

"Tell me," he said.

"I'm embarrassed," Pat said, again feeling warmth creep up her neck and onto her face. "A grown woman. A grandmother!" She breathed deeply. "I should have known better."

"Tell me," he said again.

"It's a long story," she said, "and you're hungry."

"Isn't the diner close?" he asked.

She nodded. "There's one about another mile down this same road."

He reversed his Grand Am and moved back out onto Twotown Road. "I'd rather talk about my neighbors," Pat smiled.

"That bad?" Frank asked. "Come on now. What happened?"

She took a deep breath. "I wasn't exactly the sharpest needle in the pin cushion. I fell for a big fat line like a trout goes for a fancy lure." She pointed again. "The diner is just around that curve."

"You aren't the first person to get snookered," Frank said. "Tell me."

Pat looked carefully at him as he slowed and turned into the almost-empty parking lot. He had the tan of an outdoor man, the muscles of someone who had worked hard and now kept himself in top shape. His sport shirt was softly comfortable, but his loafers looked new, as did his khaki pants. "I wish Nancy had come with you," she said.

"I don't," Frank smiled.

Pat raised her eyebrows, wondering whether he was inviting her to ask questions, but they were at the restaurant, and he was turning off the ignition and getting out of the car. Before she could even reach for the handle, he was there to open the door. She looked at Colin's best friend—and now perhaps hers. "I'm not used to this," she said. "You'll spoil me."

"You could, I believe, use a little spoiling." He took her elbow.

The diner was obviously new but had been built and decorated to look like the diners of the twenties and thirties—chrome, red leather, black metal, Art Deco silhouettes and line drawings.

"Where would you like to sit?" the bob-haired hostess asked.

"A booth," Frank said. "Corner if possible."

They sat opposite each other, afternoon sunlight cutting across the table and onto the menus the hostess gave them. "Your server will be right with you," she said as she filled their water glasses, then went to the cash register to take care of four departing customers.

They ordered soup and sandwiches, and, as the elderly waiter moved away, Frank said, "I guess Walmart hasn't grabbed up all the senior citizens. You ready to tell me about your so-called fiasco?"

She shrugged. "Not so-called. It was a bona fide disaster. At least personally."

"Did you lose a lot of money?"

"He paid every cent of what he owed me, and then some, even for the work I hadn't finished."

"The panels in your studio."

"Plus some I hadn't even started. And I kept every cent of it, that son of a —"

Frank laughed. "Good for you. What did he do for a living before the restaurant caper?"

Pat sat back and closed her eyes. The soft sounds of classic jazz—Errol Garner? Duke Ellington?—filled the room, and she remembered one day, a Tuesday, when Jamie had invited her to have lunch at his almost-opening restaurant. He had prepared the salads himself, regaling her with wine and tales of his high-seas adventures.

The music in the background had been jazz then, too, and she remembered his voice perfectly.

"The wine is one of my best," Jamie had said as she arrived, later than she had promised. "Would you prefer something different?" He had pulled the dark brown bottle from the silver ice bucket, and she could see the French name on it.

"Heavens no. It looks fine." She tried to sound worldly wise. "I'm told that wine should not be too cold."

She apologized for her lateness, explaining that she and Stephanie had gone to the fitness center. "I hadn't even showered when you called, and you certainly would not have wanted this to be a come-as-you-are party. I would have chased you and all of your crew right out of West Virginia."

Jamie sat down after pulling out her chair and running his hands across her shoulders. She had tingled all over, and even now, the same kind of thrill came with the memory.

He had lifted generous helpings of the salad onto each of their plates, then cut into a loaf of dark bread that set the juices flowing in Pat's mouth. "Made it myself," Jamie bragged, "and we'd better eat fast—I'm so hungry I could eat barnacles." He lifted his glass and said, "To my beautiful luncheon companion," and Pat swallowed hard to keep from giggling with pleasure.

"To my very generous and thoughtful host," she had managed to say. "Barnacles? I never heard of anyone eating barnacles."

He laughed at her, amusing the men installing acoustical tiles on the ceiling near them, and then he explained. "No one does, at least not to my knowledge, and certainly not the shells."

"They have shells?" Pat asked. "I thought they were like mildew or mold only bigger. Sort of like big seaweed only petrified or something."

Still chuckling, he explained in great detail, and then she asked, "How do you know so much about barnacles?"

"Two years and three months on a whaler out of Gloucester—Maine," he said, and Pat remembered him saying the words as simply as if he had said he had driven a coal truck across I-77.

"Really?" She had been wide-eyed.

"I'll prove it," he bragged. "I'll throw out some whaling terms and their definitions. You see if you can catch me in a mistake."

He had started with blubber—"It's whale fat," he said, "as hard as wood, and we cut it up into blocks about a foot square and an inch thick. We called those chunks Bible leaves. True or false?"

"You're kidding me," she said as she picked the anchovies off her salad and laid them aside.

"No, that one is for real," he said. "I'll take your anchovies." He retrieved them from her bread plate. "How about skegs—the center boards under an old whaler."

Pat had just shrugged her shoulders. How was she supposed to know that?

"Let's see—a Port Royal Tom?" Jamie asked her, and when she could not answer, he said it was a giant tortoise, the meat of which had been eaten by sailors before the animals became an endangered species. He went through try-pots and spermaceti and breaching—which she had thought meant a difficult birth—plus other terms and facts.

"Did you know," she now opened her eyes and said to Frank, "that a whale's brain is six times the size of a human brain and that whales used to grow to be 85 feet long and weighed sometimes 80 tons?"

"Good heavens!" Frank said. "How do you know that?"

Pat chuckled. "And did you know that their penises can be five or six feet long?"

Now it was Frank's turn to blush, and he did, even as he laughed. "You're putting me on."

"Nope!" She grinned. "But I'll bet you do know what ambergris is."

He nodded. "An ingredient of perfume."

"But do you know where it comes from?" she asked.

"Whales, undoubtedly."

"Their intestines."

"What?"

She nodded proudly. "When they're constipated." Frank frowned in disbelief. "Jamie told me that," she said. "He used to be a whaler."

"Aha!" Frank said. He leaned close. "Jamie is the—"

"Was," Pat corrected him. She pressed her lips together. "Definitely was. The owner of that restaurant—P. J.'s Seasonings. Porter Jamison his name is—was."

"Aha!" Frank said again. "The plot thickens. Where did you meet him?"

"He called me after he saw my ad in the phone book. He said he was opening a restaurant and remodeling it and wanted special windows." She had started the story, and now she hurried to finish it. "We got together to talk a couple of times, and I showed him pictures, and he eventually came over to Blooming Rose Court to see the doors and windows I had done, and he said money was no object, so I suggested four sets of windows that he could change with the seasons, and that's where the name of the restaurant came from, and that's how I got a contract for eighty thousand dollars. Eighty thousand dollars, Frank! Have you ever heard of such a thing? By the time it all blew up on me, I had made the sprites for spring, and I had finished the clowns for summer and a sample scarecrow for fall and a sample snowman for winter, and I had started designing the front doors."

"Wow!" he said. "How many windows?"

"Four sets of eight windows plus that big front door you saw. Thank goodness I hadn't made the doors."

"You mean he would replace the windows four times a year? Where did he get his money?"

"He said his wife had died of colon cancer about six months before," Pat reported, "and was rich and left him a bundle, and he said he had waited on her hand and foot and mouth—he said—for over a year, and just before she died she told him to do something really fun, something he had always wanted to do, it didn't matter what. So he sold their big house where they had lived for thirty years and all the furniture except his computer work station, he said, plus some pots and pans and a few towels for the bathroom, and then he bought a speed boat and then he built a little cabin on the lake, he said, and that was where he had been living. He said he wanted something else to do that would be with people because he was getting lonesome, so he looked around and saw that this old roadhouse was for sale, so he went to the bank for the money he needed, and I had done some West Virginia birds for their windows, so he looked me up in the phone book, and he called me, and before I knew it, he was writing a check for twenty thousand dollars to get me started."

"A twenty-thousand-dollar advance?" Frank said. "He was going to replace the windows four times a year?" he asked again.

Pat smiled. "Not quite. Nowadays the thing to do with stained glass is to put in permanent window sashes with special grooves for the stained glass, and then you can just snap the panels into the permanent windows. That way they can be repaired or replaced easily and they're protected by safety glass on the outside. The only problem with this new arrangement is that the safety glass on the outside can create an awful glare. But it's good protection, and it can be cleaned easily."

"Sounds clever and cozy and a fantastic idea that someone came up with," Frank said. "Too bad no one thought of that before the Reformation. We might still have some of the windows that were destroyed back then." He signaled the waiter for more water. "Had you done that kind of window before?"

"No, but it worked. I put in the first set of windows about two months ago, a couple of weeks before Jamie disappeared. They were those sprites you saw in the studio. I was working hard on the drawings for the doors—trees and birds—sort of like Stephanie's window and Dolly's French doors."

"You got all of the pieces back?"

"Yup. I've already sold some of them. Want to be my agent for the rest of them?"

"There's a thought," Frank said. "Not that you need one. You seem to be doing all right on your own."

"And you have a book to write," Pat said as the waiter approached.

He set bowls of soup in front of them, then added a basket of crackers. "You want your sandwiches now?" he asked.

"At your convenience," Frank said. "We're in no hurry." He turned back to Pat. "Tell me more about the restaurant."

She nodded. "He had already booked a big lobster blow-out for opening night, and he had hired an orchestra and he was even staying at the restaurant so he could work as late or as early as he wanted."

Another memory of another visit came to her, and again she remembered his deep, smooth voice there in his restaurant office.

"Come with me, honey," he had said.

"I believe," she replied, "that I could live on the way you say 'honey.'"

"I want to show you my cuddy," Jamie had said.

"Is that some kind of pet whale?" Pat asked.

"It's my hideaway. My cuddy-cupboard."

He had furnished a tiny room under the restaurant with a recliner, a TV set, a bar, and a bed, a very small, made-up bed. Pat had felt the warmth of the French wine, the draw of that bed, the strength of Jamie's arms as he turned to hold her, the sound of herself purring as she laid her head on his chest. And then he said, "Do you know what noises whales make?"

"I've never talked to one," she had giggled against his neck. "They won't even come when I whistle." Could she really be doing this, she wondered. The man was her employer. He was also a stranger, but he was so attractive!

"Female whales make clicking noises like this. Tck, tck, tck," he said in her ear.

Shivers had gone down her back. "And what do male whales say?" she managed to ask.

"They clang." He had pressed his body against hers, and the shivers almost took her to the too-narrow bed. Instead, they pulled apart, and they instead drove to his cabin on the lake and proceeded from there.

"Anything else?" the waiter was now asking Frank as he set down their sandwiches. All Pat could do was shake her head. Her mouth felt dry, her eyes wet.

She got through half of her grilled ham and cheese. Frank ate all of his, and while he did, Pat told him the rest of the story.

She had finished the last clown window, ready for summer, she said, and wanted to surprise Jamie, so she loaded them into her new Subaru Outback, which she chose, she told Frank, because it would hold her projects and would be comfortable and reliable. "Celia had driven my old car to the mall just the week before and managed to plow right through the loading dock at Sears where she went to buy a new mattress because she said the one on her bed wasn't good enough, and I agreed because the one on my guest bed was pretty old and I could put Celia's former mattress on it. She can be so difficult, though, such an airhead. She couldn't have gotten a mattress into that car anyway—"

"The restaurant windows," Frank smiled. "You're stalling."

Pat shrugged in agreement. "Okay. So I took two of the clown windows—after loading them all by myself—and got to P.J.'s, and it was all locked up. I drove on out to Jamie's house, but it was also locked up tight, and the boat was in the boathouse, not at the pier. Strange, I thought. Where could he be?"

She pushed her plate and the remaining half of her sandwich toward Frank, took a sip of the coffee the waiter had brought, and continued. "So I drove back to P.J.'s and pounded on the door until one of the workmen came, and I asked if Jamie was there, and he said no, and I asked him where he was. I was there to install windows, I said. The man just smirked at me and said, 'Stay here.' So I did, and then he came back, and he had an envelope in his hand, and it had my name on it, not even handwritten—just computer— and I turned it over, and it was obvious that the workman or someone else had opened it, but I didn't say anything even though the flap was all gritty and smudged. I just put it in my pocketbook and asked the man if he would help me unload the windows, and he said, 'Forget it. He don't want no more windows, lady. He is shutting this place down. That's what we're doing.'"

Pat looked at Frank to make sure he was listening. He was. "I decided," she continued, "I'd better read the letter, so I went back and sat in my car and opened it, and the letter said, and I think I can practically quote it, 'Tazewell Stained Glass Artistry, 35352 Blooming Rose Court, Tremont City, West Virginia 26111. We regret to inform you that due to changes of circumstance, P.J.'s Seasonings will be closed for an indefinite period. The balance owed you for your work is enclosed herewith. We wish you success in future endeavors.'

"Frank, that bastard never even signed the letter." Pat bit her lip, took a drink of her water, and decided to finish her story. "But he did sign the check. Needless to say, I was surprised. In fact, it was a good thing I had eaten breakfast or I might have passed out on the spot, but I decided that no man who would do a thing like that is worth fainting over or even dirtying one's clothes over—I had dressed up big-time for the surprise—so I just took a deep breath like both Colin and my mother taught me to do in distressful circumstances, and I climbed back out of my car and on very shaky legs marched back to where the workman was watching with that smirk on his face. Then I think he decided to feel sorry for me because he said, 'He screwed you, ma'am.' His very words. 'He screwed you, ma'am.' So I took another hopefully inconspicuous deep breath and asked him for any further information he might have. He said, in just about these words, 'The SOB has run out on you, ma'am.' And I just stared at him until he nodded like one of those bobble dolls and said, 'That Wanda, ma'am,' and I managed to ask him, 'What Wanda?' and he said, 'That Wanda that was always hangin' around when you and him wasn't doin' it. They was headed for her place in Key West I reckon.'"

Tears were running down Pat's cheeks, and Frank reached for her hands. "Honey," he said, "you don't have to—"

"Yes, I do," she said. "It's just so embarrassing. I was so stupid. I am so naïve."

"That's not always bad," Frank said.

Pat pulled a tissue from her pocketbook and wiped her nose. "It was this time."

"That's the last you heard of him?" Frank asked.

"Not quite," she said. "I went back home and checked my e-mail before I even unloaded the car, and there was a message from Mr. Porter Jamison. He had been sending me little love notes like 'I can't wait to see you tonight' and 'You are a beautiful answer to every question I have ever asked' and 'I love you forever.' Oh, Frank, I had even kept every one of those messages. I was such an idiot—"

"Hey," Frank said, "maybe it's a good thing—"

She offered a small laugh. "It was, in fact. I may be stupid, but I'm not the dullest knife in the drawer. The last message just said, 'Sorry.' I took copies of all the messages and that crummy notice he had left for me, and I took his check, and I went to my lawyer, and he said to go right ahead and deposit that check—fast. I could, the lawyer said, use it in any way I darned well chose, and if I wanted to, I could sue for breach of promise and get even more money."

"Are you going to?"

"I do not ever want to see him again, not even in court," Pat said. She sat up straight, wiped her nose, and squared her shoulders. "I have contacted an auction house in Pittsburgh, and I have removed the windows that were already in the restaurant, and I am going to sell all of them to the highest bidder, hopefully the one who comes the greatest distance and will get them far out of my sight—Honolulu or Perth or the South Fork of the Amazon River. As far as possible. I want the damned things out of my house and out of my sight."

"And out of your heartbeat," Frank smiled. He took both of her hands, soggy Kleenex and all.

She looked hard at him. "I am lucky to be rid of him. I have better rats to skin."

Frank laughed. "I hope I'm not included." Letting her hands go, he sat back again. "Did you have any warning at all?"

"Now that I look back on it—and I have looked back on it a lot—I did. Strange phone calls even when we were having dinner. A couple of letters that were lying on his desk addressed in a woman's handwriting from Florida, and one time when he said he was going to be out of town but I saw his car at Howie's Restaurant when I went shopping in Logan, and I almost went in and probably should have. Things like that. And last Christmas."

"What happened?" Frank drank what was left of his coffee.

"He said he was going to Key West to spend the holiday with his family. That was okay except that I wondered why he didn't invite me. He knew I was going to be alone because Celia was going to visit Roswell. They didn't invite me either. I decided I should work on the spring windows anyway, but I was miserable. He didn't even call me all that week—eleven days. I should have known, but I didn't want to. It's ironic—I had just started thinking of myself as a woman of accomplishment, a woman who could still attract an attractive man, a woman who knew who she was and what she wanted," Pat said. "And then along came Jamie." Pat smiled one-sided. "I just wish—" She was thinking of Jamie's cabin, his seductive ways.

"Let me ask you something," Frank said as he laid the tip on the table and stood. "Look at me."

She lifted her head and met his eyes.

"Do you consider me attractive?"

She chuckled. "Of course."

"See? You weren't mistaken on that count," Frank said. "You can still attract an attractive man, honey."

"Oh," she said, "I could live on the way you say 'honey.'"

Chapter 5

It was close to rush hour when they left the diner, and traffic was heavy. Frank wiggled his Pontiac between cars, around trucks, but the going was slow. Pat unbuttoned her blazer, and Frank reached behind the visor for his sunglasses and flicked on the air conditioning. She lowered the visor on her side, opened the mirror, reached into her pocketbook for lipstick, and put it on. "You haven't told me about Nancy," she said as she looked over at Frank. "Are you avoiding the subject?."

His smile was weak. "With good reason," he said. "It's not a pleasant topic these days."

"Do you have a picture of her?" Pat asked.

Keeping one hand firmly on the steering wheel, Frank reached into his hip pocket for his wallet. "In the first pocket," he said.

And there Nancy was, her expression almost grim. "She's changed," Pat observed. Nancy's hair was much lighter than Pat remembered it, and, in spite of heavy make-up, deep wrinkles were visible around her eyes and mouth. Pat suppressed a feeling of smugness as she straightened in her seat and sucked in her stomach. Nancy was at least thirty pounds heavier than she had been in Durbin.

"To say the least," Frank said. "You probably wouldn't recognize her, Pat. She's changed."

Pat couldn't argue.

"I'm sorry about that time after the funeral," he said as he wove between two cars. "I've wanted to apologize, but how can you apologize for someone else?"

"What time?" Pat asked as she tucked the photo back in and handed the wallet to Frank.

"Colin's funeral—when I called her to say I was going to stay over to help you sort some of Colin's papers."

"I don't remember." Pat shook her head.

"I offered, and you said you'd appreciate it, but I didn't stay after all. Nancy said she was sick, so I went on home." He sighed. "She wasn't, of course."

There was a long silence while they both watched the traffic. Finally, "Change of subject," Frank said. "What came before Stephanie and Tiffany and their glass? How did you happen to take that class in Logan?"

Zipping her pocketbook and replacing the visor, Pat brushed strands of hair from her cheek. "I think," she began, and then she said firmly, "I know—it was while Celia was in the hospital."

"When was that?"

"Several years ago. I'd have to look it up. After Colin died," she said. She looked at Frank. "You had moved back to Logan, but you were out of town, I remember, because I tried to call you—and I got Nancy instead. She was in a big hurry, on her way to her stained glass class, she said. You had called a few nights before to check on us, before we knew Celia was sick. She had her appendix taken out, and she almost died."

"Nancy never told me." He turned to frown at Pat. "She was taking a class?"

"I was at the Logan hospital day and night for five days because Celia's appendix had ruptured," Pat remembered, "and I was really scared, and Rosella and Roswell were just too busy to bother to come. Rosella told me it was only an appendix and said she would send flowers, which she never did. Roswell's words were 'Big deal,' or some profound statement to that effect, and when I told him Celia had come down with pneumonia besides, he asked me if they were giving her antibiotics, and I said of course, and he said, 'Fine,' and hung up. So I sat by myself next to her bed or in the chapel waiting for her to wake up or get better or whatever, every moment wondering what kind of mood she would be in." She watched as a sports car zoomed around Frank's Grand Am, then went on. "I remember praying aloud, thinking God might hear me better if it was out loud—I was very, very tired—and desperate."

She laughed lightly, "There was this snippy little intern—a girl about ten years old, I swear, who kept asking Celia how bad her pain was on a scale of one to ten, with Celia lying there sweating and gritting her teeth and barely breathing and as white as that crunchy paper they put on the beds these days instead of sheets. I kept saying, 'Ten! Ten! Ten!' I tell you, that intern was a pain herself."

She paused to let Frank concentrate on a lumber truck. "On the day that Celia was to be released," she said, "I had gone to get the house ready and put some flowers in her room, and the phone rang. It was one of the nurses, and she said Celia was throwing a fit and swearing and smashing things. I told them to give her an aspirin—which is what I had been doing for years—or a pain pill. The nurse said they had already tried that, so they had called in the staff psychiatrist and they just wanted me to know.

"Needless to say, I was back at the hospital in about five minutes," Pat reported. "The psychiatrist asked me a million questions and then said it looked like she had Bipolar Disorder, which he tried to explain to me, and that he thought it could be controlled with medication. He started her on lithium. She came home a few days later in a good mood, thanks to that medicine, and, to my utter amazement, she even noticed the roses and daisies I had gotten for her."

Two dachshunds in the backseat of the car in the right lane barked at them as Frank passed.

"She was fine then," Pat said, "but within a few days she was like a broken law of physics or something. Isn't that a neat phrase?" Frank nodded. "I don't know what it means," she said, "but it sounds good. I read it somewhere."

"What does it mean to you?" Frank asked.

"Something that isn't supposed to happen the way it happens."

"Works for me. What wasn't supposed to happen?"

"She wasn't supposed to be loving and kind. That isn't the Celia I know, not since Rosella's baby and not since Colin died. Anyhow, she was feeling so good that she refused to take any more medication, and I didn't know that I was supposed to force it on her—another broken law, chemistry if not physics, right?"

Frank braked behind an eighteen-wheeler and said, "I am so sorry, Pat. If I'd known—"

"I know, and I didn't mean to tell you all this now, but it's your own fault," she smiled. "Yours and this traffic."

"Celia got worse."

"Much. She started screaming at me, blaming me for keeping her locked up in the hospital for so long, blaming me for not letting her talk to Rosella, blaming me for the fact that the sheets on her bed at home were wrinkled. She even blamed me for folding the towels wrong. Everything she could think of. She even blamed me for Colin dying. 'You should never have let him be a damned miner,' she said. 'He was the only person who ever really loved me,' she said. Stuff like that."

"What did you do?" Frank asked.

"Put the lithium in her milkshakes and took her to see that psychiatrist." She lowered her head and clenched her fists in her lap. "Oh, Frank, I pray every day that the Good Lord will lay his healing hand on her. I dream of her like she used to be—skipping into the kitchen early in the morning, and she says, 'Good morning, Mama. I love you.' And she drinks her orange juice and tells me about the fabulous man who took her out to dinner and to a concert, and then she takes an apple and a carton of yogurt out of the refrigerator and off she goes to her high-paying job as a corporate accountant or a model or an actress—she could do any one of those things. I truly believe she could."

"Good," Frank said. "You gotta have faith, kiddo."

"I know, but just when I think things are going better, she starts talking about how worthless she is and how everyone hates her and how ugly she is and how she hates this house and how she might as well be dead. That's scary. Sometimes she leaves the house and is gone for hours, and she comes back drunk and wearing the same dirty clothes she had on the day before. Then she'll go to her room and lock the door and go to bed, still not changing her clothes, and she'll cry and cry and she won't let me in, and I sometimes hear her breaking things, even the mirror on her dresser once, and when I picked the lock one time and went in, she threatened to kill me if I did not stop interfering."

He looked over at her. "That's more than scary. That's very serious."

"I know," Pat nodded. "But I don't want to talk about it anymore right now. I worry about her constantly, to the point that I believe that if I didn't have my hair color renewed every month, I would be grayer than you are, and neither my mother nor my father had gray hair, so that's all Celia's fault. The disorder, right? But I don't want to talk about it any more."

"All right," Frank offered, "you started to tell me about how you got started with stained glass."

"I did, didn't I." Pat backtracked. "It was your Nancy and that window in the hospital chapel. And your Nancy. When I called and you weren't there and Nancy said she couldn't come because she was leaving for her class at the Celtic Center. She meant 'Civic,' of course." Pat giggled, remembering. "I'm glad you didn't see that scene. I was so excited about that chapel window and my brand new idea that I tried to tell Celia about it, and there I was telling her when she was just out of surgery, saying that the architect should have designed space in the wall of the chapel for a stained glass window."

"I take it he didn't."

"No. Probably someone donated the stained glass after the building was finished. People are like that—they don't want to get involved in anything until they're absolutely positive it's going to succeed." Her eyebrows rose. "Like I should have been before I messed with that Mr. Porter Jamison."

"The glass," Frank insisted.

"So did you know that stained glass is the only art form that is dependent upon an outside factor—light? And there in that chapel was—is—that lovely panel of iris and tulips and forsythia, a gorgeous free-standing piece with a light bulb behind it. It's so sad!"

"Celia never saw it?"

Pat laughed again. "There I was babbling on about that panel and how I was going to get into stained glass as soon as Celia was well again and how I was going to join that class Nancy was taking at the Civic Center. Celia looked up at me, in all her pain and grogginess, and she said, 'Go to hell, Mother,' but I thought she was asking for Jell-O, so I got some from the cafeteria, but when I got back, she knocked it right out of my hand and said, loud and clear this time, 'Go to hell, Mother.' I tell you, Frank, I was so tired that I just sat down in that recliner that is about as comfortable as an electric chair, and I cried until I fell asleep. But the idea for getting into stained glass, Jell-O or no Jell-O, was there to stay. And so was Celia's affliction, BD as they call it in the health business."

"A lot happened in a short time, didn't it," Frank remembered. "I still miss Colin. I wish I'd known about Celia. At least we could have brought you a loaf of bread."

Pat smiled. "Colin was special. And we would have enjoyed the bread."

"We're going to talk about Colin another day," Frank said. "Right now, tell me about stained glass—how it's made, what you do with it, what's next on your agenda. Did Nancy ever—"

Pat looked out the car window at the road sign. "She didn't. She was there the first time I went, and it was just the third or fourth time the class was meeting, and she never came back after that." Pat started to say more, then changed her mind. Frank did not have to know about the scene with his wife, how Nancy had accused Pat of horning in on the class, how she had said Pat was just trying to get to Frank, how Nancy had demanded her money back—which the instructor had refused—how Nancy had stormed out of the room, sweeping her arm across the work table, sending glass and tools and pieces of lead flying in all directions. Pat remembered now the embarrassment, the wide-eyes of the four other class members, the open mouth of the instructor as they all watched Nancy flounce out, her Aigner boots stomping an irregular rhythm as she charged down the hall and out of the building. No, Frank did not need to know about that. "How much time have you?" Pat asked as she recognized an upcoming turn-off.

"I'm planning to leave the motel," Frank said, "before dinner time. Nancy is due in tomorrow. But I'll be back soon. I'll call you."

"Can you spare another hour or so?"

He glanced at the clock on the dashboard. "Sure."

"Take the next exit—the one marked Bailey Lake."

"Where are we going?" he asked.

"I want to show you where the other half lives," she smiled.

Several twisty miles, and they were at the lake, on the road that ran beside opulent homes. Pat pointed. "That's where Celia's old psychiatrist lives. Not bad, huh?"

"Huh!" Frank grunted as he slowed and stopped the car at the side of the road. "He must have a slew of rich patients."

"Not Celia anymore. And probably most of his patients have become poor because of him. That man is a lakeside robber. He obviously does not need the money, and I'm sure he is no Robin Hood. Dr. Fancy-Schmantzy Baltry charges fifty dollars if you so much as call him to ask what time it is, which of course nobody does, and he's always on vacation, in which case his receptionist refers you to another psychiatrist, and you get charged to talk to the receptionists at both offices because the second psychiatrist is also on vacation, and by the time you can find anyone to help you, the seizure has passed and you've wasted another couple of hundred dollars."

"How can you avoid it?" Frank asked.

"I kept a record," Pat said, "of anything Celia did that was not absolutely normal, and I sent it to the doctor by e-mail. He charged me only for the time it took him to read it and answer it—at which time he almost always said, 'Be sure she takes her medication and bring her in.' My e-mails were cheaper than taking her to his office and sitting there for three hours every other day, but it was still a rip-off." They watched a chipmunk skitter into a hole at the base of a nearby tree. "She usually refused to go anyhow. But then she got onto what Dr. Baltry called a plateau, and he said she might stay that way for a long time. She's definitely not what he calls 'ultradian,' which means extreme mood swings every single day. He thinks she's an 'ultracycler,' which means extreme moods for less than a week at a time and infrequently, thank goodness. But there's a third kind that I wish Celia was—a person who has these extremes only every few years. Then she could hold a job for a while—provided," Pat laughed, "she didn't get mixed up with any more homosexuals. I'll tell you that story another time." She touched Frank's arm and hurried with her story. "You would have laughed at her—well, maybe not laughed— when I suggested the other day there was a 'Help Wanted' sign in the McDonald's window. She got really nasty, saying that she wasn't well enough to work. I told her all she would have to do was put her finger on the right computer picture and charge whatever the computer told her to charge. She could manage that, I said."

Frank chuckled. "She loved that one."

"She told me that since I was the senior citizen in this household, I was the perfect candidate for McDonald's. I'd fit right in. Or I could try Walmart because I would look cute, she said, grinning like a senile illiterate and shoving carts at people."

"I don't think so, honey," Frank smiled. "Stick with your glass." He was looking up at the Baltry mansion. There was a guard dog on alert at the top of the long driveway, a Doberman, no less. "This place could house fifty homeless people plus a dozen unwed mothers and their sixteen children," he said. "Bipolar Disorder can't be cured?"

"It's believed to be a chemical imbalance, so it can be treated with drugs like lithium, but it's typical of Bipolar Disorder people to think they're cured, and they stop taking their medicine, and then, like when Celia was in the hospital, they're in trouble."

"How did you learn about—BD? She still takes lithium?"

"Plus some kind of anticonvulsant because there's a theory that the switches in mood are caused by brain spasms. I talked to some people, including a doctor that Susan Lefler interviewed on Public Radio, and I check the Internet constantly in the hope that some new treatment has been developed." She looked at Frank. "Would you believe— Google comes up with over two hundred thousand websites." Frank gasped, but Pat did not wait for him to speak. "And the word 'bipolar' isn't even on my spell checker! Naturally, I haven't gone to all of the sites. One of them was listed as treatment for heartburn and BD. Forget that one. Another site, though, described a BD person as being a psychic suicide bomber."

He turned in his seat to look at her. "And you've been living with this all this time?"

"It wasn't really bad until that episode in the hospital, but as I look back, the symptoms started after all the other members of our beloved little family were gone and Celia and I were alone. She doesn't like me much, so that makes it very hard for her."

"For her?" he asked, eyebrows raised. "What about you?"

She shrugged. "There isn't much I can do except try to get her to take her medicine, and I pay the bills—like one time she came home with a fur coat for me and four pairs of Clark shoes for herself and a dozen other packages from Nordstroms, and there was a truck right behind her with a giant TV to deliver. Why, he couldn't even have gotten that thing through our front door." She laughed. "Anyhow, that's euphoria—the 'high'—when you think you own the world. Severe depression is much worse. At least I could return the coat and the TV."

"What happens?" Frank asked.

"Suicidal tendencies." Pat spoke matter-of-factly. She saw that the watchdog had lain back down. "Sometimes she just disappears, and I finally find her in some bar or some alley or sitting on the bank of the river. Sometimes she just locks herself in her room. That's the easiest."

Frank took his foot off the brake and pulled up into the steep Baltry driveway. The dog leaped up and began barking, but it stopped as soon as Frank backed off. "We're probably being recorded on a surveillance camera," he said.

"Like on NYPD Blue," Pat said, "and our Dr. Baltry will wonder who with a Pennsylvania license plate was about to break into his humble abode. That should keep him occupied for a minute or two. You'll be on his hit list. Don't turn around, though. Keep going," Pat suggested.

"It says 'Private Road,'" Frank reminded her.

"Very private," she said. "The next place belongs to Mr. Porter Jamison. I want you to see the scene of my downfall, his little so-called cabin."

Frank looked sideways at her, then asked, "Are you sure? Where was he from? What did he do before the restaurant—before or after being a whaling pirate?"

She lifted her chin and tightened her mouth so as to sound haughty. "Upper Montclair, New Jersey," she said. "He grew up next door to Telly Savales, just a few doors—estates—from Olivia Dukakis." She returned her head to a normal position and lowered her voice. "Honestly, though, you'd never know it. Jamie always talks nicely to even the cleaning lady at the restaurant. I'm not sure what he did before. Real estate maybe. Yes, that's what he said. Real estate."

Frank laughed as he viewed the huge log building they were approaching. "Real estate like in *The Godfather*. He can afford to be nice. Tell me about the inside."

"A great big living room, a game room, a huge patio in the back, half a dozen bedrooms which I never saw, half a dozen bathrooms, most of which I never used, and," she pointed, "a three-car garage in which he keeps not only his Jaguar and his Taurus—which is what he drives when he deals with us commoners—but also a 1927 Chevy that's in perfect condition."

"I hope he has good security like your doctor friend."

"Oh, he's secure all right. You should see the furnishings," Pat said. "All antiques or custom-made, all of which I hope get stolen or burn, and lots of velour and polished wood and very subtle lighting. Big fireplaces. Big sofas and upholstered chairs. And a humongous copper-lined kitchen."

"How many servants?" Frank asked as he looked down toward the boathouse.

"I don't know," Pat said. "There was no one else around when I was there."

"Often?" Frank asked.

"Twice," Pat said. "Twice too many. I wish—" She stopped. "Let's go," she said.

As they drove back toward town, Pat said, "I've told Stephanie all about Jamie. And now I've told you. And you're going to tell me, like she did, to forget him. Stephanie says, 'What you need to do,

Patricia, is think about his faults.' She says that will help me regain perspective. The trouble is, he seemed so perfect." Pat sighed.

"Honey," Frank said, and again Pat loved it, "find one of his enemies, like his contractor or his lawyer—or other women. Under all that money and all that slickness, this Jamison character is probably pretty seedy. He definitely has clay feet—big clay feet."

"He talked about a lot of friends," she said, "and they sounded like really nice people," Pat said.

"Sounded," Frank said. "Did you ever meet any of them? Go for enemies, someone who hates his guts.. Brag about him to an enemy or two. You'll find out he has a hundred flaws."

"Then I'll feel like even more of a fool for believing in him," Pat said. "I even tried to talk to Celia about him because she knows a lot about men, but she wasn't interested. Bipolar people tend to be very self-centered."

"Then talk to Jerry," Frank said. "Or me." They turned into Blooming Rose Court.

Roswell's Explorer was in Pat's driveway. "Celia's sure to be back soon, too," Pat sighed. "Oh, I hope her job interview worked out. I hope she wowed them. Would you like to renew your acquaintance with her and meet my charming daughter-in-law?"

He shook his head. "I've got to go," he said, "but I'll call you sometime tomorrow." He smiled as he helped Pat out of the car. Taking on what he believed to be a psychiatrist's tone, he said, "Make sure Celia takes her medicine and let me know if Mr. Jamison shows up. We'll sic Nancy on him."

Laughing, Pat reached to kiss his cheek, then moved toward the house.

Opening the front door quietly, Pat could hear Roswell and his wife arguing. She sincerely hoped they would not decide to come downstairs. This had been too good a day. She went to the kitchen, opened the refrigerator, and pulled out a Diet Coke.

Rebuttoning her blazer and opening the sliding door to the patio, she imagined the swing as being still warm from Frank's body and hers, and she sat down. How good it had been to see him again! She looked toward the house nearby. "Jerry, buddy," she whispered, "I miss you, but Frank's a good substitute."

Ten seconds later, she heard the garage door open. She got up and, as she came around the side of the house, she saw that Celia was not putting the car into the garage. Instead, she had pulled onto the driveway and had gotten out and was lifting something out of the hatchback. "Mama!" Celia squealed. "Look what I got!"

As she came forward, staring, Pat saw not one tree, but several good-sized saplings spilling from the back of the car.

"Aren't they great?" Celia called. She was tugging at the burlap surrounding the roots of a large tree, a ficus.

"What in the world?" Pat asked.

"Trees," Celia said. She looked feverish, over-excited.

"What for?" Pat asked, her stomach tight.

"Our yard, of course," Celia said. She was grinning, jiggling up and down. "We are going to plant them between us and those filthy-mouthed animals next door."

Pat glanced toward the neighbors who, she was sure, could hear every word.

"And birds." Celia grinned even wider. "Blooming trees attract birds and butterflies and bees, and we need bees to pollinate the world."

"Celia, sweetheart," Pat said as calmly as she could, "we're not allowed to plant trees. It's in our contract. Only the development association can plant trees. The bees will have to figure out how to pollinate without us. I'm afraid we'll have to return your treasures."

"Mother," Celia said, her hands on her hips, her cheeks crimson, "you have diddly-squat—zilch—for a backbone. The hell with the damned development association." Still in her good gray suit, she dropped the ficus onto the driveway and ran high-heeled into the garage and came back out with a shovel.

Panicking, Pat said, "Celia, at least change your clothes. Are you out of your mind?"

Celia stopped in mid-stride, one foot in the air and the other wobbling to hold her up. She stared at Pat, and Pat could almost see the elation leaking out of her daughter and onto the cement. Celia's shoulders sank, and her breasts drooped, and the skin on her face sagged. Swallowing hard, all Pat could think of to say was, "Celia, did you get to the interview?"

Too late, Pat realized that that, too, was a mistake. Celia crumbled. She was like a rag doll coming apart at the seams. She sat down there on the driveway with her arms around the ficus tree. "No," she wailed. "No, no, no."

In spite of quiet pleading, in spite of begging and tugging, Pat could not get Celia upright. She went into the house and called up the stairs to Roswell. "Please! I need help," she called.

There was no answer.

Pat ran up the stairs. She knocked. "Roswell, Celia is sick. Please!"

Pounding on the door, Pat finally got an answer. "Call an ambulance," Roswell yelled. "We're napping."

Fury ran through Pat like fire. "Roswell!" she shouted. "Get out! You and your damned jewelry get the hell out of here. Get out of my house!" Pat ran back downstairs.

Celia was still sitting in the driveway. Pleading in vain one more time, Pat rushed across to the Morrisons' house. Stephanie was at home. The baby was asleep. Priscilla was at a playmate's house. Stephanie came, first running next door for Dolly.

The three of them did get Celia into the house, into the living room and onto the couch. Dirt from the trees was staining Pat's beige carpet, but she ignored it, not knowing what to say to her two friends except, "Thank you. Thank you very much."

It was Dolly who said, very business-like despite her ragged sweat pants and Bengal t-shirt, "What's going on? You need to do something about this, Patricia."

Her usually cool forehead glistening with perspiration, Stephanie patted Pat's arm and said, "Dolly is right, dear. This is beyond us. Celia needs serious help."

All Pat could think of to say was, "She just needs to take her medicine. We can help her."

"What's wrong with her? What kind of medicine is she taking? It doesn't seem to be doing much." Dolly said. She was standing with her legs astride, as if she were about to take on the Pittsburgh Steelers. "Do you want us to take her up to bed? Whose car is that out front?"

Ignoring Dolly's questions, Pat looked down at Celia, who had lain down and was almost asleep on the couch. "She'll be okay now," Pat said. "I think I should make some coffee."

In the kitchen, Pat told Dolly the truth. With Stephanie's help, she was just finishing her story when they heard Celia sobbing. She was awake and sitting up, her cheeks streaky with tears and dirt. "Honey," Pat said as she knelt on the floor in front of her and put her hands on Celia's knees, "It's okay. It's okay. We'll keep the trees. I'll talk to the association. Have you taken your medicine?"

Celia seemed not even to hear her mother. Wailing and rubbing her hands up and down her face until she looked like a Munch painting, Celia kept sobbing.

"I'm going to call an ambulance," Dolly said.

Pat leaped up to stop her. "That would only make her worse," she begged. "Please. She just hasn't taken her medicine." Pat ran to the kitchen, coming back with two pill bottles and a large glass of water. Celia clamped her lips together and glared.

"Let me get Walker," Dolly suggested as she looked for a telephone. "He's at home."

Before Pat could stop her, Dolly had run out of the house. Within minutes, Walker was in Pat's living room, and he was squatting before Celia, and he was placing the pills on Celia's tongue, and he was holding the glass of water for her, and she was drinking.

"She'll be all right now," Stephanie assured Pat, and sure enough, Walker was stroking Celia's tangled hair, and he was talking quietly to her, and soon she was lying back down on the couch and was sound asleep.

Walker stood, his thick brown hair mussed, his narrow face with its neatly trimmed beard relaxed and confident, and he said simply, "Let her sleep here for a while. Call me if you need help getting her

to bed later. You could cover her with an blanket or something."
Stooping to get his tall frame through the door, he left. So did Dolly.

Stephanie, her hand still on Pat's arm, said, "I have to go—the
baby—but Pat, call Dr. Baltry. I think Celia needs more help than we
can give her." She, too, left.

They were right, Pat conceded. Celia needed serious help, but
"Dr. Baltry is out of the country until Monday," his answering service
said. "May we refer you to another doctor?"

Pat hung up. She called up the stairs one more time. One more
time there was no answer. She went back out to the kitchen and sat
down at the table. Celia would refuse to go to a new doctor. Maybe,
though, she wouldn't have another episode for a while. Maybe. Pat
picked up her cup and drank the rest of the cold coffee. If only
someone could tell her what to do, something that Celia would accept,
something that Pat would not feel so damned guilty about.

The longer she thought about it, remembering each of Celia's
nasty outbursts, dreading more ficus trees, more midnights searching
the alleys and the river banks, the more alarmed Pat became. Shaking
with desperation, she looked up Rosella's number and called. Surely
family meant something. The phone in Boston rang twice, and then,
to Pat's surprise, Rosella answered. Even as she wondered what her
daughter now looked like, Pat said, "Your sister is worse. I need your
advice."

All Rosella said was, "Do what you think best, Mother. We
cannot get involved."

Someone was playing a piano in the background, playing one
phrase over and over. Perhaps Sty was taking lessons, but this was
hardly the time to ask. "I thought I was thinking best when I called
you," Pat said, her mouth dry with anger. "I guess I was mistaken."
Please God, she added to herself, don't let me make Rosella any
madder at me than she already is. "I'm doing the best I can for Celia.
I thought—"

Rosella's frosty reply was, "You're doing too much for a woman
your age, Mother. Do you have someone to cut your grass?"

The anger was gone, just like that. Pat laughed out loud. "Cut my grass?" she asked. "Wash my windows? Screw my screws? Oh, my beloved daughter, thank you so much for the suggestion. I'll be sure to let you know how Celia responds to your sterling wisdom." Pat lowered the receiver into its cradle.

Checking to be sure that the noise had not awakened Celia, Pat sat down at the kitchen table, put her head down on her arms, and prayed.

Then, too tired even to change clothes, she pulled off her blazer and went to her studio. For two hours she drew designs for windows. Church windows. Yes, she decided. If the congregation would pay for the supplies, she would make a stained glass window to replace the bathroom-type glass that was currently in place behind the baptistry. As soon as she got rid of the pixies and scarecrows that were cluttering up her life, she would make some real windows for the church, Stephanie's and Jack's church and now hers and maybe someday Celia's. In fact, she decided, she would pay for the supplies out of that rat Jamie's money. Perfect! Penance and revenge wrapped up in one gorgeous window.

No. She raised her head. Vengeance is mine, said the Lord. There had to be a better way. She had other money. Jamie's pay-off would take care of Celia's bills. The church window would not be contaminated by him. She would use her own money, the money she had earned here on Blooming Rose Court. Stephanie and Jack would help.

By the time Pat realized what time it was and went back to the living room; Celia was not on the couch. Her shoes were still in the middle of the floor, and the couch and carpet were smeared with dirt, but Celia had managed to get herself upstairs and into bed.

Yes, Pat discovered, Celia was sound asleep in her bed. Her stained clothes were on the bathroom floor.

As she bent to retrieve a stray towel, Pat glanced into the mirror over the sink. Oh, God, there was that old woman again. Her eyes smarted, and she took a deep breath. Oh, how she needed some of Jerry's wine! She stared at herself. Then her mind and face cleared, and she said to the image in the mirror, "Madam, some things around here are going to change or I will really start looking like you." She used the towel to wipe off her smeared mascara. Yes, some serious help for Celia. Yes, Roswell out the door. Yes, a call to Steamboat Springs, Colorado.

Tossing the towel and clothes into the hamper, Pat marched back down to the kitchen. She took the phone from its hook and, checking the numbers she had scribbled down that morning—had it been only that morning?—, she pressed eleven buttons. Jerry did not answer, but she left a message. When Pat went back upstairs to wash her face, she saw a new light in her eyes. Stephanie and Jack and Dolly and Walker were right across the road. Celia would get help. Frank was going to call in just a few hours, and Jerry would call back the minute he got her message. She lived in a lovely house in a good neighborhood, and she had enough income to live on, and she had talent, and she had a brand new project to work on. Forward, Patricia Tazewell, forward!

Chapter 6

Pat was three-fourths asleep, already dreaming about Frank and Colin playing in a scrub football game back in Durbin, when she was awakened by voices in her backyard.

Boys' voices. Lots of boys' voices plus a familiar blast of acid rock. She got out of bed and crept out onto the balcony. Leaning over the railing, she saw in the beam from her patio sensor light Tony, the Fauraults' thirteen-year-old, and Melvin, their eleven-year-old, plus three other teenaged boys. "Asshole!" one yelled. "Pucker peter!" another screamed. They were shoving each other, kicking, and fists were flying.

"Stop it!" Pat shouted over the music, and all action ceased. They looked up at Pat, who, in a moment of joy and absolute confidence, had put on her Superwoman pajamas. One of the boys, not a Faurault, adopted a falsetto tone and yelled, "Will ya look at that, fellas! Superwoman eighty years old, hanging over a balcony like a retarded Juliet. Oh, Mama! I'm scared! You think she'll jump?"

They were all laughing, pointing up at her. They began to run around the yard, following Tony, their leader. They clapped their hands and shouted, "Jump! Jump! Jump, old Juliet, jump!"

Pat looked toward the house next door. Where were Chloe and Tom? Couldn't they hear? Why weren't they out here? She peered down once more at the frenzied boys, then went back into her bedroom, turned on the lamp on the table, and picked up the phone. Chloe answered, her voice muffled. "Your boys—," Pat began.

"I know," their mother said. "I hear them."

"Can't you—," Pat began again.

"I'm sick," Chloe said. "The baby—"

"Where is Tom?" Pat asked. Through the open door to the balcony, the shouting became even louder.

Then Pat's bedroom door opened, and Roswell barged in. "What in the hell is going on?" he asked. "Who in God's name—it's the middle of the night!" He stumbled through the room and onto the balcony, and yelled, "What the hell are you doing?"

Pat told Chloe, "Send Tom." As she hung up, she heard one of the boys holler, "Oh, baby, she's got a boyfriend, a big, fat, ugly boyfriend."

"He's no Romeo," another voice came, "He's Frankenstein's baby brother."

Raucous laughter. More four and five and seven-letter words. Roswell came back into the bedroom and glared at Pat. "These are the kind of people who live here? These are your lovely neighbors? Will you please do something?"

"I didn't choose them," Pat said. "Their father is coming."

"Well, you are welcome to them and all the other perverts you hang around with," Roswell announced. "We will be leaving in the morning." He tripped on the bottom of his pajamas as he left Pat's room.

"Now, that's a piece of good news," Pat said aloud.

She slipped, now in a bathrobe, back out onto the balcony. The boys had quieted down and had crept far enough into the woods to make the sensor light go out. Pat could hear them, calling softly to each other, coming up into the edge of the yard making some kind of noise, but she could see only dark forms moving back and forth. And then one of them came too far into the yard. The sensor light came back on, and Pat gasped. The boys had gathered up branches and rocks and dead leaves, everything they could lay their hands on, and they had thrown all of it up into her well-groomed yard. "Oh, God," she whispered, and she looked again toward the Faurault home. Damn! Where was their father?

She saw one of the boys creep around the side of the house, his oversized jeans dragging behind him, and then she heard the garage door open. The radar from an overhead plane? No—there was no sound of a plane. That boy—it had to be a Faurault—had somehow figured out the code or had bypassed it and was in her garage.

Pat raced down the stairs and through the kitchen and into the garage. Tony Faurault was there, and in his hand was the flashlight

Pat kept on the windowsill in case of emergency. He had turned it on and was facing her, holding the light under his chin, making his face a grotesque mask.

Pat snapped on the overhead light and rushed at Tony. She grabbed his shoulders and started shaking him so hard that the flashlight fell from his hands and she could hear his teeth rattling. "You little hoodlum!" she shouted in his face, "Get out of this house and get out of my yard, and don't you ever come back or you will be eating your teeth."

She let go and realized that the other four boys were all at the door. She glared at them even as she knew that if they all came at her, she would have no chance. She grabbed the shovel Celia had wielded earlier, and she moved toward the boys. "Get out," she growled. "Get out," she said again. "Get out!"

Tony led the way. "Oh, hell," he said to the co-conspirators. "This is a drag. Let's split." He swaggered. "I'm going home." He and Melvin moved off toward their house, and the other three wandered off into the darkness. "See you tomorrow," one called, and another one called back, "Yeah, see you tomorrow, Mrs. Juliet." Laughter.

Her hands hot, her feet cold on the cement floor, Pat watched, and sure enough, the Faurault boys were going into their house by the basement door. There was a light on upstairs—Chloe's bedroom, no doubt.

Pat put the shovel back in the corner, pressed the button to close the automatic door, went back into the kitchen, and called Chloe again. "Where is Tom?" Pat asked. She could hear the baby crying.

"I'm sick and the baby is sick, and Tom is running in a marathon somewhere, and," Chloe coughed, "please let us get some sleep."

"Let you get some sleep?" Pat said. "Your sons have been having an orgy in my backyard, and they have left a terrible mess, and I'm sorry, Chloe, but if the yard is not cleaned up by tomorrow night, I am going to call the police." She hung up.

Roswell was standing at the top of the stairs, his pajama top tight across his stomach. "Mother," he said, "this is more than we will tolerate."

Pat snorted as she pushed him out of her way. "Then don't. You have mooched as much as you are going to. You are no longer welcome in my home. Solve your own problems, Roswell. And don't come back until you do."

Roswell's tone softened. "Oh, we're going, as I recently suggested, but—," he paused dramatically, then said sarcastically, "—you surely wouldn't turn away a son in need. There may be a time—"

She spun around. "Try me," she said. "You show up again asking for handouts, and I will call the police. And," she took a deep breath, "while we are waiting for them to arrive, I will take you sightseeing— the New River Gorge—and I will take you to the center of the tallest bridge in West Virginia if not the world, and I will encourage you to jump off—with a bungee cord if you're a good boy." She turned away.

"But, Mother," he said, his tone softer, his words slower now. "I'm your only son."

She could taste the disgust in her mouth. "You want help from now on," she said as she went back into her room, "try McDonald's. Celia tells me they're hiring."

He followed her, pajamas legs dragging. "You have never wanted us here, have you. You have never wanted Rosella and me at all. It's all Celia, Celia, Celia. You never loved me. Or Rosella"

"Oh, Roswell," Pat sighed as she turned to face him. "Get real." She closed her bedroom door in his face. Thank God, she thought, neither Marietta nor Celia had shown up.

By the time she showered again, put on clean pajamas, and crawled into bed, the sun was coming up and Jerry was calling.

"What time is it out there?" she mumbled.

"Five on the clock Colorado," he said. "Up and at 'em, kiddo!"

She sat up against the headboard of her bed. "I've been up and at 'em all night, Jerry. All night."

"What you mean?" he asked.

"Your old neighbors. Those delightful Faurault kids. They've been raising hell, mostly at my expense. You should see my yard. All those flowers you and I planted? They're ruined."

"They drinking? Doing pot weed? Where is their mama and papa?" Jerry asked.

"Ha! Winning another damned trophy somewhere, and Chloe is in bed."

"You call the police?" Jerry asked.

"I didn't, not yet, but next time—heaven forbid there should be a next time—I will indeed. And if they don't clean up— What are you doing up at this hour?"

"Sorry about yesterday, kiddo," Jerry said. "Me and the boys rafting on the Yampa. You will love it, so much fun. Today we go fishing. Colorado trout is best in the world. When you coming to taste it?"

Pat took a deep breath. "I'm going to do that, Jerry, but first I have to put Celia in a hospital and kick my son out of this house."

"Oh, my goodness," Jerry said. "Celia very sick?"

"I'll tell you about it later." She yawned. "Jerry, I have to get some sleep. Can I call you tonight?"

"Sure, kiddo. We will be back—," he paused, thinking, "—eight or nine your time. You sleep. Ciao, kiddo."

But of course she couldn't sleep. Instead, she dressed and went down and began pulling Roswell & Company's leftovers from the refrigerator. Like the hospice, she would not hasten their demise, but neither would she prevent it. By the time she had cleaned all of the shelves, she heard activity above her. Heck, she thought, she could afford now to be generous, so she set the table for four—perhaps Celia would be awake enough to have breakfast with them and say good-bye to her brother. Pat stirred up a batch of biscuits. Those in the oven, she put bacon on the griddle and opened a carton of eggs. Sure enough, as the odors drifted up the stairs, down came Roswell and his wife, each carrying a large cardboard box. Neither said a word, however, but went out the front door and pushed the boxes into the back of their Explorer. Leaving the door open, they trooped back upstairs, back down with more cargo.

This happened four times before they descended with suitcases and garment bags.

Pat heard the front door slam. Then she heard a car engine and the screech of tires. Pulling the griddle onto a cold burner, she got to the sidewalk in time to see Roswell's tail lights go around the curve toward the interstate. Then she gasped. The cats! What in God's name was she going to do with three cats? And Roswell couldn't possibly have gotten all of their cargo into that car. They would be back.

Pat stood there for a moment and then let out a long sigh. Of course she loved her son—if not also his wife. Of course she wished she were on better terms with him. Of course she should have tried harder to please them. But three cats? All that junk jewelry?

Here we go again, she thought. She had spent her whole adult life trying to please her children, her childhood trying to please her parents and her brothers and the math teacher and the cheerleading and track coaches and about seventeen would-be girlfriends. She had not really been that cute, happy, oh-so-popular Patsy Yokum. She had been a struggler, a second-best, the girlfriend of that also almost-invisible Fonzie O'Connell.

That real Patsy Yokum must not come back to haunt Patricia Tazewell, Artist in Stained Glass. Yes! That old Patsy Yokum had just gone around the curve toward the interstate. That Patsy Yokum was sitting meek and complacent in the back seat of an overcrowded Ford Explorer, trying not to displease anyone in the whole wide world.

This Patricia Tazewell, by damn, would not house three cats for very long!

She continued to gaze toward the interstate. Then she blinked her eyes. Was she seeing things? Her imagination had been working double-time overtime, but this was real. Coming around the curve and away from the interstate was Frank O'Connell's Grand Am. It came to a stop virtually at her feet, and out climbed Fonzie. No, Frank. "Good morning, Mrs. Tazewell," he said. "How about a Belgian waffle at IHOP?"

She grinned and moved to take his hand. "No IHOP in this neighborhood, Mr. O'Connell, but there are homemade biscuits just about to come out of the oven at that place on Blooming Rose Court."

They went inside, Frank's arm warm around Pat's plaid-shirted shoulder, hers warm across the back of his golf shirt. "I thought you were going to call," Pat said. "This is a wonderful surprise."

She led him to the orange juice and bacon and biscuits and eggs, and as she poured his coffee, he said, "I hope you'll forgive me, sweetie, but I couldn't think of anywhere I would rather be today. You too busy to spend one more day with an old buddy?"

"Never," she said. "Not if you're up for church."

"Thought you might suggest that," Frank said. "I have a jacket in the car."

She sat down and offered him the platter of eggs. "Nancy didn't get home?"

He grimaced. "Oh, yes. She's home as of last night. Same old same old. Her plane landed early, and I wasn't there. Need I say more?"

Pat's eyebrows rose. "That's all? You just weren't there when she landed?"

"That was more than enough. She didn't let up even after I said I was going to bed. Followed me upstairs and filled me in—again—on what a lousy husband I am, etc., etc., etc. I finally just got up and dressed and threw a jacket and toothbrush into the car and headed out."

"Won't she worry? Where did you sleep?"

"No and no," Frank smiled. "She'll be fine, and I'll catch up on sleep tonight."

They sat in silence, eating. Finally Pat brightened. "I have an idea. Let's go to church, and then let's drive up to Durbin if you're not too tired. We can prowl around there, and we can talk about Colin and the old days for your book, and we can see if the Double-D B&B is still in operation, and I'll leave a note for Celia, and—"

Frank leaned back in his chair, grinning. "That is the greatest inspiration you have had since stained glass." He leaned across the table and took her hands. "You look a little sleep-deprived yourself, young lady."

"Understatement of the day," Pat said. "Tell you what." She looked at the Mickey Mouse clock on the wall. "The early service is at eight-thirty. What the kids used to call 'Big Church' isn't until eleven. It's just eight now. We could both sleep for a couple of hours."

"If I slept now, I wouldn't get up until tomorrow," Frank said, "and I don't want to miss today."

"Me, too—I'd never get up." She turned her hands over to hold his. "I have to tell you what happened last night, and I have to clean up the mess Roswell and Company left behind. We'll go to Big Church."

"They're gone? What about Celia? Will she go with us?"

"She slept through all the excitement, probably won't wake up until later. She had a busy day, but that's another story. We'll leave her some biscuits. She'll be all right for today. I'll ask Stephanie to stop by this afternoon."

He helped clear the table and fill the dishwasher, then went to the doorway. "You have any carpet cleaner?" Frank asked. "It looks like your living room needs some help."

"You shouldn't have asked. That's another whole can of mealy worms." She stepped back to open a cupboard under the sink and pulled out a can of Woolite and a sponge mop. "I hope this works," she said. "Know anyone who wants a cat or two?"

Leaving him to deal with Celia's dirt spots, Pat climbed once more to the second floor. The room Roswell had been occupying looked just as Pat expected it to—stained sheets, over-flowing wastebasket, smudged mirror, food-smeared bedspread. Holding her breath, she stripped the bed, rolling all of the laundry into the bedspread. Down to the clothes washer. Back up with Windex and furniture polish. Struggling, she managed to turn the mattress, then left the bed uncovered to air, cleaned the rest of the room as well as she could without waking Celia in her room across the hall, and joined Frank on the back patio. He was staring at the trash in the yard. "What went on here last night? Motorcycle gang? Earthquake?" He paused. "Not Roswell."

Pat chuckled. "Not quite, although he participated as a spectator and commentator. Let me change clothes and I'll tell you everything on the way to church. Need anything?"

"I'll make another pot of coffee. You can drink some on the way."

As she passed through the living room, Pat turned and called back to him, "You're magic, Frank. The rug looks like new."

"I'm not so sure. The motorcyclists got inside?"

Once more up the stairs, one more change of clothes, this time into blue corduroy pants and jacket and a pair of loafers—they would be going on to Durbin, she reminded herself. A touch-up in the bathroom, and she was ready. She made a quick call to tell Stephanie she would meet the Morrisons at church.

As she sipped the hot coffee in the car and pointed directions, Pat told Frank about the Faurault boys and their friends. As she ended the story, he asked, "Where are these people from—not that it matters?"

"Chloe is from War, West Virginia." She giggled. "Maybe the boys have taken the name of their mother's hometown seriously," she said. "Chloe was teaching in Pittsburgh, though, when she met Tom at a race. They were both runners back then. She isn't anymore, not marathons and stuff like that. She was an English teacher, which probably also accounts for her kids' behavior. After teaching junior high English, even a saint would throw in her halo."

"Her husband?"

"Long Island—which probably explains why they don't get along very well. Different worlds growing up. Tom's an accountant, and I think he's pretty good, but he works for other people and is constantly getting fired because he's always off to the races. He does come home with trophies or medals. That's the only time he speaks to the neighbors—to show off his latest win. That's another reason for Chloe to give up on her boys. Their father is never at home, and she has a new baby, and both she and the baby are always sick. Or so it seems." She paused. "I guess I should feel kind of sorry for Tom. His whole identity is wrapped up in his running. What's going to happen if he breaks a leg or a dog trips him or something? He's no Lance Armstrong, bicycle or no bicycle."

Frank grunted. "Sounds as if someone should, in fact, trip him up. What are you going to do about the backyard? I could clean it up for you."

"I told Chloe the boys have to clean it up or I'll call the police."

"Good."

"There's the church."

Ahead of them on the right was a simple red brick building with a typical black signboard in front of it. "Middle Creek Baptist Church. Worship 8:40 a.m. and 11:00 a.m. Sundays. Bible study Wednesday 7:00 p.m. Ralph Sandusky, Pastor."

"What brand of tongues do they speak in your church?" Frank asked.

"Strictly English," Pat said, and then she corrected herself. "Plus a couple of Hispanics who speak Spanish to each other, and a Slavic family that speaks excellent English to us, Slavic to one another. It's American Baptist.'

"Was that what your church in Durbin was?" Frank asked as he parked along the side street.

"Independent. Freewill. Bible-thumping. Long hair, long dresses, and very long sermons. You'll like Mr. Sandusky. He stopped by my house within a week after the first time I came to church with Stephanie and Jack. Celia had had one of her spells and was in her room, so I sneaked him past the living room and into my studio, and," she said as she opened her car door, "he liked my work. He stayed long enough to help me clean the cement from part of the Marlinton window. You'll like him."

"I will if he's married."

"He is—and so are you," she added. He grunted.

On the sidewalk, she looked at her watch and then up at Frank. "Still fifteen minutes, but we can go in. Everybody will be in Sunday School classes, including Jack and Priscilla. He brings her, and Stephanie comes later with the baby, but he says he's going to keep coming. He's a good man even if he is a dentist."

As Pat had predicted, the sanctuary was empty except for a few choir members shuffling music and zipping up robes. The plaster walls had been painted pale green, and the carpet was a darker shade of the same color. Light oak pews filled the two sides of the room. At the front was a platform, on one side of which were pews for the choir. On the other were the pulpit and electronic organ. At the center back was a space which obviously contained the baptistry, and in front of it was the communion table graced by a large bouquet of gladiola and carnations. "Nice," Frank said.

Pat stopped in the middle of the aisle. "See that ugly window behind the baptistry, the one that looks like a shower stall?"

Frank laughed quietly as he drew up beside her. "You're right."

"It's got to go," Pat said, "and I'm just the person to get rid of it."

He looked at her with raised eyebrows.

"A memorial to Colin," she said. "I decided last night. I'm going to do a window based on the river in Durbin—where Colin was baptized."

Frank looked steadily at her. "That," he said, "is a great idea."

Impulsively, Pat asked, "Would you like to help?"

He turned and put both hands on her shoulders. "I would be honored," he said.

"It's tedious and dirty and cruddy work," she said, "but I'll bet you wield a wicked soldering iron. You could do that."

"Just my cup of whatever—lead?" Frank asked as he took her elbow and led her to a pew. "Let's just sit a minute."

They did not speak for several minutes. Then Pat put her hand on Frank's, and she said, "Your coming to see me is a true-blue miracle, Mr. O'Connell. You're making me realize that I've been running around like an eye doctor with a beam in his—her—own eye. You've taken it out for me. It had the initials 'P.J.' burned into it. Jamie's."

"I thought Jerry was doing that, removing the beam, I mean."

She nodded. "I have to give a little credit to Jerry and Stephanie and a smidgen to Dolly, but you've helped me focus. I feel as if a few of the tangled webs around me are beginning to untwine. I can't tell you—." Pat couldn't finish.

He laid his arm along the top of the pew behind her shoulders.

"Tell me about you Baptists. I'm something of a Methodist."

"You could do worse," Pat smiled. "There are all kinds of Baptists. Like the church back home was Freewill. They weren't connected with anyone or anything else." She touched the cover of the Bible in the rack in front of her. "Biblical. Literal. And then, sort of at the other extreme, there are Baptist churches that are practically Episcopal or Presbyterian. That's what Stephanie has told me, anyhow. She knows everything about Baptists. This one is sort of in between."

"So what do Baptists have in common, if anything?" Frank asked. He nodded to the usher who had brought them copies of the program.

"Believer's baptism, baptism by immersion, the priesthood of the believer—and open communion, at least most of them."

He turned his hand to hold hers. "No sprinkling."

"No sprinkling—although I guess sometimes people who have been sprinkled can be Baptists later, maybe even without immersion."

"Immersion because of John the Baptist and Jesus? And no popes, no bishops, no cardinals," Frank said.

She nodded, enjoying the warmth of his closeness, the smell of his aftershave. "We think," she said, "you can talk to God yourself without help from anyone else."

"I think everyone believes that, down deep. I do—and I was born Catholic, like Colin, and then went Methodist—like Nancy."

"Colin used to tease my mother about being a Dunker," Pat said. "That's what he called us, and that's what people called the people who went to the Church of the Brethren back home, too. Remember?" She looked up at him. He seemed so solid, so comfortable, such a perfect fit with her new self.

"I remember I used the term on him one time," Frank said, "and he almost punched me out. What about your kids? Celia?"

Pat shrugged. "She used to like church, but she hasn't been going since we moved, since the BD got worse. I just keep hoping. As for Roswell, I think he goes, Episcopalian, I think." She smiled. "He needs someone to tell him what to do. I sure can't." She reached to shake the hand of a woman entering the pew in front of them.

"He's gone," Frank reminded her as they both watched people straggling in and sitting in pews in front and to the side of them.

"Thank God," Pat said. "I literally thank God." Her smile disappeared. "But I wish—"

"I know," Frank said.

"As for Rosella," Pat sighed. "God only knows. Literally." She paused. "I just hope she is raising Sty to be a Christian. Preferably not Catholic."

Frank chuckled. They both turned as someone behind them said, "Pat?" It was Stephanie, her long blond hair shining, her red dress perfectly pressed. She had a fussy baby in her arms. "I'll be right back," she said, "provided Tracy goes to sleep in the nursery." She smiled at Frank. "Good morning."

"She's a psychologist?" Frank asked as she hurried away and the organ prelude began.

"Social worker, like I told you," Pat whispered. "She goes to people's houses and tells them how they can improve their lives. I'm not sure how she decides where to go, probably her boss, someone at the Department of Health and Human Resources. That's who pays Stephanie. But from what she tells me about where she goes and the people she sees, she is not paid enough. The people she sees are really tough, and I think it's dangerous."

"She's not exactly a stereotype of a social worker."

"You'll like them," Pat said. "Jack has a great sense of humor. You'll have to ask him what he does for a living. He'll tell you he runs a filling station."

"Clever," Frank said. "Dentistry is another profession I would not want to be in. Ugh!"

Pat snickered. "Better than a urologist," she said. She pulled a piece of paper from her pocketbook, a long annotated list, and showed it briefly to Frank. "My prayer list," she said, "in case the sermon gets boring." She held it long enough for him to see the names of her children, her neighbors, several people he did not know.

The pew beside them had filled, and, although Stephanie had not returned, Pat pointed across the aisle and whispered, "That's Jack.

He drove past us yesterday. I'll introduce you after the service."

The organist finished a Mendelssohn prelude, and the choir filed in, their burgundy robes swishing as they slid into place. Across from the musicians, Ralph Sandusky climbed onto the platform and sat down behind the pulpit. Pat moved even closer to Frank and closed her eyes. "Oh, yes," she murmured. Frank squeezed her hand.

Hymns, prayers, offering, sermon, benediction. Pat hadn't had to pull out her prayer list. The service ended, and Ralph Sandusky stood just outside the door, greeting the sheep of his flock. "Good morning," he said as he shook Frank's hand, the one not holding Pat's. Then Sandusky turned to Pat, took her free hand, and said, "You're looking lovely today," and he winked. "Peace and blessings."

"And to you," she said, winking back.

They waited on the sidewalk as Jack and Stephanie, Priscilla and Tracy came toward them. The baby was crying enthusiastically. "Sorry we can't stay," Stephanie said after introductions. Her hair was still perfectly brushed, her dress still clean and unwrinkled. "He's having a bad tummy day."

Jack, slightly more disheveled than his wife, swung Priscilla up into his arms and said, "My girl and I are having a good tummy day, but we're running on empty, aren't we, Princess. Good to see you, Pat. Come over later?"

"We're off to Durbin," Pat said, "our growing-up ground. Would you mind calling Celia later, just to be sure—"

"No problem," Jack said. "Go dig up your past."

As Pat and Frank moved toward his car, Priscilla turned and waved. Over the buzz of conversations around them, they heard her high-pitched "Nice to meet you!"

"She's a doll. Durbin," Frank said as he opened the door for for Pat.

"Durbin," she agreed.

Chapter 7

"Stephanie is beautiful," Frank said as they drove out of town.

"I know. She always makes me think of Talbots. Have you seen their TV ad, the mother and little girl looking in the window of an antique store and oh-h-h-ing and ah-h-h-ing over a porcelain statue of a ballerina?"

"I thought you said it was a Talbots ad. Isn't that clothing?"

"Right. In the ad these two are wearing fancy-schmancy Talbots clothes like three hundred dollars' worth each, and the little girl goes back to the store later—maybe with her father—and buys the figurine for her mother. Yeah, sure, just an everyday occurrence in Durbin, West Virginia."

"What has that to do with Stephanie?" Frank asked as he headed north with the light traffic.

"She's Talbots all over, and so is Priscilla. They could be the models for that ad, and I'd be jealous as hell," Pat laughed, "except that she has practically saved my life." She sobered. "You know, I think that's true. I thought moving to a new house in a new neighborhood and all would be enough, but Celia—well, it wasn't quite as peaches-and-cream as I expected."

"Lonely?"

"Not exactly. I've never been much of a social butterfly and I really have been enjoying my studio and all, but Celia—well, she hasn't been exactly supportive, and she sure isn't happy."

"Would she rather have stayed in Logan?" Frank asked.

"That's what she says, but she was unhappy there, too. I think Celia would be unhappy anywhere. And she blames me."

"And then along came Stephanie," Frank said as he went around a Sunbeam truck.

Pat smiled. "Along came Stephanie, and she is at least as much of a daughter to me as Celia is. And Jack and Stephanie have let me share Priscilla and Tracy, sort of be a surrogate grandmother."

"Where are the real grandparents?" Frank asked.

"Jack's are divorced. His father lives way up in northern Michigan and tracks wolves and thinks Jack is just a money-grubber, which he is not, and Jack's mother has remarried and lives in Malibu with a movie writer and has sort of disowned Jack because she doesn't want her new friends to know how old she is."

"You're kidding!"

"Straight up. And Stephanie's folks are both dead. Killed in the crash of a private plane. They had won a trip to Nova Scotia, some kind of a raffle or something, and were with another couple, and they had all hired a private plane to fly them around the area, and it crashed in the ocean near Halifax."

"Terrible! How long ago?" Frank asked.

"Years, maybe ten." Pat sighed, leaned back, and closed her eyes. "Before Stephanie and Jack were even married. She was still in college."

"Well," Frank decided, "I'm glad she has you for a substitute mother—or big sister." He paused, then asked, "Do you know how to get to Durbin from here? I never even looked at the map."

"Actually," Pat said, "you can't get there from here."

"Good. We'll just keep going," he laughed. "Just nowhere near Pittsburgh."

She shook her head. "There's no good way, but we can go up to Flatwoods and then wiggle our way across to Route 219. That will eventually get us there."

"I like the wiggle part," Frank said as he maneuvered himself into a comfortable position and adjusted his seat belt. "Tell me when you get hungry."

"We can stop in Flatwoods," she said. Leaning over to check his gas gauge, she said, "You can fill up there, too."

He pressed a button, and National Public Radio came on, Fiona Ritchie and her "Thistle and Shamrock" music filling their mini-world. "Tell me what you do other than stained glass and Celia and—whatever."

She opened her eyes, pondered a moment, then said, "Workout

and hospice stuff and yard and now church and, most recently, Bunko."

He turned to look at her. "You're hospice. Your shirt. Me, too. Bunko?"

"You'll love the Bunko bit. Stephanie and Jack moved in, and it was obvious right away that they were churchy people—they'd leave the house by eight every Sunday morning and wouldn't get home until almost two. Then they'd leave again about six-thirty, and they'd come home about nine. They also went to Bible study on Wednesday nights, and they'd go out again on Thursdays with a baby-sitter for Priscilla, and I just assumed they were going to choir practice or visitation or something. Stephanie belongs to some kind of women's group that meets twice a month, and she's on a couple of committees and so is Jack. But," Pat paused for emphasis, "I was wrong about Thursdays." She pointed to a hawk circling above them. "Have you ever heard Colleen Anderson's hawk song?" She sang part of it for him, ending with her favorite line—"And when I am with you, no matter the place, I'm riding the wings of a hawk."

"That's wonderful," Frank said. "She should record that."

"She did. Does. Sometimes with Kate Long. You've heard Kate—probably Colleen, too—on West Virginia radio. When we get back," Pat said, "I'll play a couple of their CDs." The hawk had disappeared above the wooded hills.

"Thursdays. Jack and Stephanie. They were not shopping at Target," Frank suggested.

"Huh! Far from it. Jack and a bunch of other men play poker at each other's houses every Thursday. For money. Not much, like nickels and dimes, Stephanie says, but money just the same. And I don't believe the nickel and dime part even though Stephanie does, because men are just not nickel and dimers. Women, yes. Men, no. At least not in Durbin and not in most coal towns, not the men I've known. They're beer and bucks."

"Not me," Frank argued.

"You're an exception," Pat smiled. "Lots of exceptions."

"So where's Stephanie while Jack is anteing up?"

"Would you believe? The wives get together to play Bunko, and," she said slyly, "I've gone a few times, and you absolutely will not believe what goes on at those parties."

"Try me," he said. He pressed the accelerator as they approached the access to I-79.

"Well, I go, and I don't play very well because I am completely distracted by the behavior of a couple of the women who start drinking early and keep going."

"Drinking too? Whee!" Frank laughed.

"Like this one woman," Pat continued, "whose name is Mary Louise but who acts more like a Trixie or a Desiree. The more she drinks—hard stuff that she brings with her—, the fouler her mouth gets and the fewer clothes she has on. It would really be kind of disgusting," Pat said, "if she weren't so funny. She tells the dirtiest jokes God ever created, although I seriously doubt that dirty jokes are created by God. More likely people—or the Devil, if he is able to create anything." Frank pointed to a doe above the highway. Pat nodded. "At any rate," she continued, "Mary Louise means no harm, and her jokes really are funny, and the parties are harmless even if Mary Louise does get so drunk she can't sit down, let alone stand up. She's the worst one, but it is not at all unusual for Stephanie and me, neither of whom drinks anything but Diet Coke because of the calories and being Baptist, to have to take several of the women home. They leave their cars wherever the party has been and go back for them the next day."

"You and Stephanie are the only sober ones?" Frank asked.

"And Katherine," Pat added. "She doesn't even drink Diet Coke. Just water. She's diabetic and allergic to artificial sweeteners, which is pitiful, but she does tell good stories."

"And they all go to work the next morning?"

"Most of them don't work except at home. I guess they get the kids off to school on Fridays and go back to bed. I haven't asked. I've only just started going, and I'm not sure for how long I'll do it. It gets boring after a while."

"Doesn't sound very boring to me," Frank chuckled.

They decided to stop in Elkview for gas and the bathrooms, then got back in the car. "Next stop Flatwoods for something to eat," Frank said. "In the meantime, keep me awake. Tell me about Stephanie's work," Frank suggested. "Her clients and how she has time to work with you on the glass."

"She just started glass a couple of months ago, shortly before Tracy was born, and she had time because she had just dismissed three of her people, one because the family has settled down and seems to be doing better, the other two because they were making no progress after months of Stephanie's counseling." She pointed to the license plate of the semi that had just zoomed around them. "Utah. I guess this guy thinks he's still driving the salt flats. Next thing you know, he'll be over the side of a mountain."

"Probably. So Stephanie isn't working now," Frank said.

"Not since she dropped those three clients and transferred two others so that she could have the baby. I just hope she doesn't ever go back." Pat licked her lips. "Picture our perfect little Stephanie. She goes to this trailer where the man comes out and has three fancy motorcycles in the shed in the yard, and of course he wants to show them to her, and he and the woman who Stephanie is supposed to be seeing are divorced, but he's still living in town and comes by now and then to pick up one of his bikes, and while he's there, he beats up whoever is home at the time, including the kids."

"Why isn't he in jail?" Frank asked.

"Because no one will press charges, and the kids lie for him. So does the woman because she's afraid of him and his brothers, who live in the same trailer court."

"Why aren't the children taken away from her?"

"Because they're old enough—like twelve and fifteen—to say they don't want to be. Besides, this woman is a college graduate, believe it or not, and her father is a golfing buddy of the magistrate's."

"Stephanie is well out of there," Frank agreed, "and you're good for her."

Pat missed his last comment. "And then there was this other family," she continued, "with three daughters, and two of them have babies that are living right there in the house with everyone else. The two older daughters are working, and their mother takes care of the babies. That part is going relatively okay. Stephanie says it's the third daughter she worries about. What kind of a life does she have? The mother of those three is only thirty-seven years old and has had at least three husbands—or mates. Nobody even knows for sure who fathered the three girls. They just use their mother's maiden name. And what about those babies growing up in that place?"

Neither Frank nor Pat spoke again for a moment. Then Pat said, "I'm sorry Stephanie had to sort of desert them, and she worries, but it's better for her—and Jack and the children."

Frank turned a sharp curve and braked as they went down a steep hill. "So tell me, lady, in addition to Bunko, what other secrets do you have up your sleeve?"

"I have to go to the bathroom again," she said.

Their last stop was in Flatwoods, and it was evening before they arrived in Durbin. "We have a problem," Frank said as they came into town. "We can go back over those roads after dark or we can stay overnight. I vote for overnight."

Pat was quiet for a moment, watching an old man walking toward them on the other side of the street, a portable oxygen tank slung over his shoulder. "That's Charlie Simmons, isn't it?" she said. "He's a lot older than I remember."

"So are we all," Frank said. "He's a rare one, though, a miner who hasn't died of emphysema. My dad did, yours, too."

"When I was eleven," Pat nodded. "By the time you and I were teenagers, all of the women were widows because all but one of the mines had shut down and almost all the living men had moved away. I grew up on the farm, you remember, but Mama had to sell it and bought that house we turned into the B&B so that she could support my brothers and me." She paused. "I guess we can stay around here tonight," Pat said at last, "but I'll have to call Stephanie and ask her about Celia. Maybe she could get Dolly or Walker to go over."

Frank handed her his cell phone.

"Do you want to call Nancy first?" she asked.

"I won't need to. She won't really care." He pulled over in front of a deserted shoe store and waited for Pat to finish her call. Frank gestured toward another empty building. "That was Sullivan's."

"We used to buy all our groceries there," Pat said. "I wonder where people go now."

"I'll bet there's a Walmart around the corner," Frank laughed.

"Dear God, I hope not," Pat said. "Let's look for our beloved old Double-D."

"I only vaguely remember your brothers," Frank realized. "What ever happened to them?"

"Moved away the minute they could."

"Why did your mother stay?"

"You must remember. Durbin was turning into a ghost town, and then, all of a sudden, a lot of publicity showed up about the radio telescope in Green Bank, and everybody started talking about the fancy things that were being done to the Cass Scenic Railroad, and Durbin got to be known as a quaint little place to visit. So people visited. There wasn't much to stare at here except Mama and me and the football team—you guys—but Green Bank and Cass were close by, and then they started building Snowshoe."

"That's become quite the place," Frank said. They watched two boys come zooming by on their skateboards. As soon as they had passed, Frank pulled away from the store and drove down the street. "I was there for a conference last year," he said. "It was so foggy we couldn't see from one building to another, and I wasn't impressed with the lodge I stayed in, but it was one of the oldest ones. The newer ones are better."

"Did Nancy like it?"

"She didn't go," Frank said.

"There it is!" Pat cried. She pointed. "Oh, my gosh, there it is!"

The old house still stood on the corner where it had always been. The sign was new, but it still said "Delightful Durbin Bed & Breakfast." "Oh, Frank, let's stop," Pat cried.

Apparently in response to the sound of their car, a young woman came out onto the porch, her hair in a braid down her back, her jeans and blouse clean, her feet in heavy leather sandals. They climbed out of the car and went up to meet her. Yes, she said when Frank asked, she had one room available for the night, a twin. Without even asking Pat, he said, "Fine. Any chance of a cup of coffee while we rest our bones on your porch? We're both originally from here, and we've come back to reconnoiter. And look for food."

"I'm Jessie Miller," the woman said, "and I have a casserole in the oven. If you'd like, I'll fix you some supper right here on the porch. Not many other possibilities in town on Sunday night. Ready in about twenty minutes." She went back into the house.

Names and places and events rolled off their tongues as they sat there looking over the wooden railing. "Remember?" Pat would say, and then Frank would tell his story. "Remember?" he would say, and it would be Pat's turn. Within half an hour they had resurrected at least fifty people and the events to which they were attached.

When Jessie came out and began setting two places at the pine table, Pat asked, "Would you and your family like to join us? Have you other guests?"

"No other guests. I had hoped to finish remodeling all of the bedrooms by the first of June, but yours is the first. And thank you, but I'm not married. No family, no guests except you."

"Join us," Frank insisted.

She did, and Pat ate little as she told Jessie the whole story. "Mama made all the new curtains after we decided to be a B&B," she said. "And we refinished a bunch of furniture—the dining room table, for instance, and I did all eight of the chairs. Mama recovered the seats. We bought most of the other stuff at auctions or people gave us things so we could get started, and I washed every blessed dish that had been in the house for centuries, and we bought a pile of new ones at the general store in Petersburg—no Dollar Store back then. And we had the bathtub reglazed, and I waxed floors, and Mama dug the gardens and planted zinnias and Dusty Miller, I remember, because the deer were supposed not to be interested in them, but nobody told the deer that."

"How long did you live here?" Jessie asked as she spooned another helping of lasagna onto Frank's plate.

"Five years. More than five years."

"By yourselves," Jessie said.

"My brothers took off for Ashville or wherever they thought the coal was not as dirty or you could get it without having to dig. I lost touch with them a long time ago." Pat turned to Frank. "Do you remember them now?" He nodded. "They both took off," Pat told Jessie, "the day Billy John turned sixteen, and Mama had baked a great big fancy cake that he never even saw, and she cried for hours. They never came near again." She laughed. "Not even to borrow money. Not only ungrateful but pretty stupid. Mama would have paid them to come home."

Jessie frowned at Pat. "What was your maiden name?"

"Yokum."

Jessie shook her head. "I thought maybe I had met your brother, but it must have been a different guy. I'm pretty sure his name was Billy John, a man in Mars Hill." Her frown deepened. "He was the one who told me about Durbin and about this bed and breakfast, but his last name wasn't Yokum. He was working at the college, on maintenance."

"How did you meet him?" Frank asked.

Jessie smiled. "I worked for the college, too. I taught physics."

"And now you're here?" Frank asked. "Durbin?"

"Seemed like a good idea," Jessie said. "I hated teaching college kids. They think you'll give them a degree if they just pay enough money. And most of them are on financial aid, so it isn't even their money." She shrugged. "It wasn't like that twenty years ago."

Pat's eyebrows rose. "You were teaching twenty years ago?"

Jessie smiled. "Student. Anyhow, this man told me about Durbin, and I came, and I liked it here, and I intend to stay forever." She rose. "If the Bed and Breakfast doesn't get going, I'll apply to teach high school math. That has to be better than dealing with spoiled college kids. Let me get you some dessert and more coffee."

Pat turned to Frank. "Weird—two men in North Carolina named Billy John."

Frank scraped the last of the lasagna from his plate and licked his fork. "Willie Joe, Bobby Ed, lots of double names in these parts. Maybe Jessie will remember his last name. We could find out what it is."

"Why?" Pat asked. "I have no interest in Billy John Yokum or Billy John by any other name." She looked out at the deserted street. "I just keep thinking of Colin and all the fun we used to have. And some of the sadness."

"You know what?" Frank said. "I have an idea."

"Don't tell me you want to move back here."

His eyes narrowed as he looked at her. "Would that be so bad?"

"Yes," Pat said. She accented every syllable. "I do not want to live in the past."

"But," Frank said, "there are a lot of good things about the past that ought to be remembered. Like Colin and that fun we had. We don't have to move back. I'm going to write about it, and you're going to help me."

"I can tell you stories."

"You can write them."

She stared at him, then said, "Look at me, Frank. I am not Patsy Yokum anymore. I am Patricia Tazewell."

"You are Pat—Patricia—Yokum Tazewell, widow of Colin Tazewell, and you are now living in Tremont City, but you were born and grew up and lived a big chunk of your life as Patsy Yokum in Durbin, West Virginia, and you have stories to tell."

"So do you."

"Of course. I can write my stories, but it would be great if you could write some of yours."

Jessie was back with a carafe of coffee and a plate of mint brownies. "Oh, my gosh," Pat said, "those are Mrs. DeMott's cookies."

Jessie frowned. "I found the recipe in the back of a drawer in the kitchen. It looked like it came from a magazine."

"It did," Pat laughed. "I had forgotten all about it." She turned to Frank. "You won't remember Mrs. DeMott. She was only in town a year or so and then moved up—up, mind you—to Morgantown. She brought these mint brownies to our Christmas party one time, and I asked her for the recipe." Pat wiggled her shoulders and tipped her chin up. "She just stuck up her nose and said, 'I never give out recipes,' and I was absolutely humiliated. Then just a couple of Sundays later, there was the recipe in the newspaper. That just tickled Mama and me to death. We made some and took them to her, pretended we had forgotten all about her precious Christmas cookies."

Jessie chuckled and set the plate down. "I'm just glad I found it. I'll bring more coffee in a few minutes. I'm going to have to get back to work."

After Jessie had departed, Frank said, "I'm going to the car, and I'm going to get us some paper and a couple of pens, and we are both going to write, lists, things we remember, places we used to go, people we went to school with—whatever."

"I can't—" Pat began.

"You can," Frank said, and he hurried down the stairs, pulled his briefcase from the trunk of the car, sat in the driver's seat for a moment, then came back. "Tell you what," he said. "You stay out here, and I'll go in the living room, and we'll both scribble down whatever pops into our heads. One hour. Then we'll compare notes."

Pat looked out over the porch railing again. Just down the block she could see the empty Sullivan store. Beyond it were the houses that the Reillys and the Nortons and the McDaniels had lived in. Just beyond that was a video store that had once been a pool hall, the pool hall that Colin had gone to after dinner here at the Delightful Durbin. A block farther on was the grade school, and there were two girls swinging on swings that had probably been there when Pat and Fonzie were their age. And somewhere just out of sight was the Freewill Baptist Church where Pat had learned to sing "Jesus Loves Me" and "How Great Thou Art." She closed her eyes, then opened them again and reached for the coffee pot. "Give me that paper," she said.

Frank grinned and handed her a pad of lined yellow paper and a ballpoint pen. "Think Colin," he said. Tucking his briefcase under his arm, he picked up his cookies and coffee cup and headed inside.

When he came back out two hours later, the porch light had come on, and the street beyond the house was dark. Pat was swatting at mosquitoes, but she was still writing. She looked up and smiled, and Frank could see tears glittering in her eyes. She put down her pen. "I don't know whether to thank you or kick you where it hurts," she said.

"Colin," he said. "Let me read it?" he asked.

"You'll have to. I certainly can't read it to you." She handed him her yellow pad.

Frank moved his chair to where the light seemed best, and, in his deep, strong voice, he read aloud.

I was eighteen, one month and three days out of high school, when my whole world changed forever. Mama and I had been running the Delightful Durbin for four years, all the time I was in high school, and I was wondering whether I would be changing beds and washing dishes for people from Baltimore for all the rest of my life. But that day was the last, at least as far as feeling stuck was concerned.

I was bringing a French Lady from the oven. (That's a sort of soufflé that Mama and I made up and sent to Betty Crocker and got a year's subscription to *Good Woman* for.) I was just putting it on the side board (*Good Woman* said we should call it our buffet), and down the stairs came this guy staring at me, and in spite of the fact that the pan was hot (and so was I), I stared back. Mama was right behind me with the rolls, and I heard her whisper, "Oh, my stars, I am going to lose my Patsy."

She was right. Colin Tazewell had been sent to Durbin by a British coal company (also by God, I think) to see if any of the mines around Durbin could be reopened. He was from Cardiff in Wales, and he had black, black hair and blue, blue eyes and was so handsome that I just couldn't stand it. And when he smiled, well, you could just forget about anything else.

We got married exactly ninety-one days and seven hours after I burned my hands carrying that French Lady for his very first West Virginia breakfast, which included Mama's biscuits and sausage and the strawberries that I had picked right out of our Delightful Durbin B&B garden. (I always had to watch for copperheads out there but only ever saw one.) Plus coffee, of course, and whipped cream that came from our very own cow, Thomas Q.

Colin had to tell the people in Liverpool (?) that Durbin was pretty much worked out, but then he got a different job with a different company and he moved to Logan, and so did I after we got married.

We bought a little trailer and later a little house about five miles from the mine, and with all my experience, Colin said, I should open a catering service, so I did, and I hired young girls to help and also Celia when she got big enough, but she hated it and Rosella and Roswell were never big enough. And the girls I hired got so good they were going to start their own business, but I sold them mine instead at a nice profit and focused on raising Celia and my twins and loving Colin.

Celia was very little of a problem, not too bad at that time but R & R (who were conceived when we went to New Mexico so that Colin could see other kinds of mines and we could have a vacation and that's why Roswell was named Roswell and Rosella was named Rosella because it matched) were problem-laden, a lot like my brothers, so it may be their mutual genes which were definitely not inherited from my dependable, hard-working mother, but my father was a good man, too, and very sensible, so I don't know where that came from.

R & R were giving me fits, and Mama was getting tired of the B&B, so she sold it and came to help me with the catering until she died of a heart attack at 4:11 p.m.on May 23 in the middle of a wedding reception, very suddenly and, thank God, without pain. She was fifty-six, so I have already outlived her by six years.

Colin worked for Consol Coal Company for multiple (about 20) years, all the time saying, "I know it, Patsy. I am going to die in the mines. My daddy did and I will, and it will happen when I am forty-seven because that is how old my daddy was." And every evening before he went into the mine or sent the men down in (he had only one woman miner ever, and he always believed she was bad luck—Welsh people are very superstitious and so are all the other miners I know—so that poor woman never had a chance of not being bad luck) he had a little prayer meeting and read a little Scripture to the men. I still have that coal-stained Bible which he carried in his pocket down on the mantrip that fateful morning. It was lying next to his body when they found him crushed between a coal car and the wall of the mine. That car's brakes had let go and then that car jumped the track down at the curve where Colin got pinned between it and the wall. He died on the way to the hospital, and he was three days short of being sixty, and his hair was still black and his eyes were still blue and his Welsh accent was still like the day when he ate French Lady and flirted with me, but his chest was crushed flat as a slab of slate. I miss him, four years and three months later.

I miss him.

When Frank looked up, there were tears in his eyes, too. "That's beautiful," he said. "I do, too." He wiped his eyes with a finger. Then he looked at her. "I have also missed you, Pat."

She bit her lip, then reached for his handkerchief and wiped her own eyes. "I've missed me, too," she said. "And you. What did you write?"

He smiled. "Do you remember that Christmas when you and I and your mother went up the hollow to deliver packages?" She frowned. "That's what I wrote about," he said.

"I thought we were supposed to write about Colin," Pat said.

"We were, but I had something else on my mind, so I just went ahead with it."

"Read it to me," she said. He did.

When I was a kid, there was a company store just outside of Durbin, near the mine so that when the men got paid in scrip, they would be right there in the store. Quite often the women would be waiting to make sure that the scrip was spent on things the family needed. I remember seeing my own father just hand his pay to my mother because they both knew that if he didn't, he would spend it on moonshine or worse and we would have to go hungry until the next pay day.

The company store carried everything from bags of oranges (only at Christmas) to work boots to buckets of lard to school notebooks. The mine owners probably made half of their income off of what was sold at the company store.

We got to go to the Cass store once a year, however. Cass was where the steam-engine train would carry logs down off Cheat Mountain, and at Christmastime the train would come up loaded with special things for people to buy for presents. I remember ugly ties for the men who never wore ties except for funerals. I remember ruffled aprons for women whose day-to-day aprons were made from flour sacks. They saved the ruffled ones for when the preacher came for dinner. And I remember bushel baskets full of toys made in Japan which broke within five minutes of our first trying them. We could peek in and see the insides of those toys, most of which were made from Prince Albert tobacco cans, and I always wondered how anyone could have loved Prince Albert, that man with the long, scraggly beard. I had seen pictures of Queen Victoria, and she was no prize, but I thought she surely had more choices than that ugly Prince Albert. I remember wishing I could have one of everything in that Christmas-happy store, but I knew I would be lucky to get new shoes and an orange.

But my favorite Christmas of all time occurred when Patsy Yokum's mom invited me to go with them to spread Christmas cheer. I had loved Patsy ever since second grade, and now we were fifteen, and I was seriously thinking of asking her to marry me. I remember my little brother Paul teasing me about Patsy and asking me if I was going to have kids with her, and when I said I was thinking of it, he said that he would like to have some kids someday, too, but he didn't want to have to do what you have to do to have kids. I told him he would change his mind about that.

Anyhow, Patsy's mother was in the front seat, and Patsy and I were in the back with bags and baskets of food and toys under our feet and beside each of us so that we were sitting very close together, and I was in absolute heaven. We went up the hollow and then down near Logan into Holden, which was also known as Holden No. 22. Many coal towns, like this one, were named for mines. Century No. 2 is another example up in Marion or Harrison County—up there somewhere.

We delivered the baskets to the doors of poor people, and on the way back when I still sat close to Patsy even though all the baskets were gone, Patsy's mother got to talking about what had happened recently in Holden when a woman named Mabel or Margie was murdered and thrown down over a hill on Trace Mountain because the murderer thought her body would never be found. It was, by a kid picking blackberries, probably the very next day. According to Patsy's dad, an innocent man was sent to jail for life because the woman was really shot by her husband. She had been hanging out on Stratton Street, notorious in those days even among us teenagers, and she had a list of lovers as long as a mine tunnel. Everyone knew, according to Patsy's mom, that her husband had killed her, but he and the big shots in Holden were all buddies, so they sent an innocent man to prison, and the case was closed.

That was the Christmas I spent with Patsy Yokum sitting very close in the back seat of her mother's car, my favorite Christmas ever, complete with murderers.

Pat stared at Frank, not able to speak.

He reached for both pads of paper and Pat's pen and tucked them all into his briefcase. Then he stood and took her hand. "Come on. We both could use some sleep."

"Shouldn't you call Nancy?"

"She called me. There were two messages on my car phone."

"Is she all right?" Pat asked.

Frank grunted. "I'm surprised you couldn't hear her from here."

"She's mad."

"You could say that."

"Should you go home?" Pat asked.

"That's not what she's mad about."

"What then?"

Frank grunted again. "She couldn't find her tickets to a concert at Heinz Hall tonight."

"Do you have them?"

"She thought I did, but she called back. They were right where she put them—on the piano."

"Why was she mad?"

He laughed. "Because I didn't have them and they were right where she left them, and I didn't answer the first call when I could have told her where they were and she wouldn't have missed the concert. Come on. Bedtime. No strings attached."

They took turns in the bathroom, Pat first, and by the time Frank came out in his undershirt and shorts, Pat had pulled off her slacks and shirt and had crawled into her twin bed in her underwear. "Good night," Pat said. "I guess."

"You guess what?" He asked across the narrow space.

"I guess—I guess—"

"You guess you shouldn't come over here."

She chuckled. "I know I shouldn't."

"Why not?"

"Because—." Her voice faded in the dark.

"Because Colin is still filling that space," Frank said.

"Sort of," she admitted. "I guess he always will be."

"At the moment maybe," Frank said. "We've been talking about him. But he's gone, Pat. Don't let him—"

"Good night, Frank," she said again.

He sighed. "Good night."

Both of them actually slept well.

Chapter 8

They were up by six the next morning, and while Frank went for a quick walk, Pat showed Jessie how to make French Lady. "It's so special-looking but so simple," Jessie said. "Everybody will love it." While her two current customers ate, Jessie went back to work on her remodeling and redecorating.

"I'd better call Celia," Pat said.

"She's all right, honey," Frank said. "Let your surrogate daughter do the mothering."

"Once a parent, always a parent," Pat said. "But you're right. Stephanie can handle her."

"When do you absolutely have to be back?" Frank asked.

"I wish I could say never. Suppertime will do."

"I remember a couple of other Christmases here," Frank said without warning.

Pat stopped her fork in mid-air and looked at him. "So do I." She took a deep breath. "Mama and I always made decorations after school and in the summer, and whenever we didn't have a houseful to cook for, we were making ornaments and decorations. When I was little they were paper chains, stuff like that, but," she said, straightening her shoulders to look proud, "they weren't just ordinary paper chains. I cut the paper with Mama's pinking shears. When I grew up, I graduated to Styrofoam ornaments with sequins and pearl beads and ribbons. They were stuck together with tiny pins."

"I remember you always had a present for anyone who showed up at your door," Frank said. "Like us strays."

She smiled. "Yeah—an extravagant present like a jar of jelly or a painted cardboard picture frame—or one of my ritzy-fritzy ornaments."

"Or a pair of hand knit socks," Frank said. "I wore mine until they literally fell apart, and I still have one of those ritzy ornaments.

And a hot pad you made for my mother. And a cardboard frame with a picture of my favorite cheerleader in it." Pat was staring at him, so he added, "Everybody loved Christmas here, and it got so everyone in town stopped by, right?"

"Thank goodness, everybody also brought fancy breads or cookies."

"But they could never out-fancy you and your mother," Frank said. "My mom wasn't much of a cook, so she always brought along a smoked ham or a chicken, whatever she could scrounge up."

"I remember!" Pat said. "You both were so generous. Everyone in Pocahontas County was." She reached for one more biscuit. "What about your mother?"

"Mom died of cancer a couple of years ago. Brain tumor. Slow and painful."

"I am so sorry!" Pat said. "I wish I'd known. Was she in a hospice?"

"There wasn't one. That's why I started one, as a memorial to Mom and Dad. We cover most of Pittsburgh now."

"You're kidding!"

He smiled. "That's what I do instead of knitting socks. That's my fun."

"Fun?" Pat asked. "I'm a volunteer, too, but it's not exactly fun."

"Of course not."

Jessie appeared. "Will you be able to stay for a few days? I'd love to have you." She smiled particularly at Pat. "I need some more good recipes."

"I'll send you some—after I write them down. Ours were mostly hit and run, wing and a prayer, seat of our pants, guess-and-by-golly— that kind."

"We'll have to be leaving soon," Frank said. "After one more cup of coffee." He stood and stretched, then followed Jessie in. He brought a carafe and filled Pat's cup.

They were back in the car and cruising around town by eight o'clock. "There's Babe's house," Pat would say, and then Frank would say, "There's Wild Bill's Garage. I wrote a poem about him once."

"Really? I want to read it." And then Pat said, "Didn't the post office used to be in that building?"

And then Frank said, "There's the old football field," and he slowed the car. "I remember busting my butt to impress you. Many an opposing player is still sporting a crooked nose or a bum knee because of you, my love."

Pat, her cheeks burning, turned to look at him. "We were very good friends, weren't we?"

"More than that," he said slowly. "You were my ideal, my goddess, my end-of-the-rainbow. Patsy Yokum, that redheaded cheerleader. Every male kid—no, females, too—thought Patsy Yokum was way beyond perfect, the absolute model for what kids today would call 'way cool.'"

Pat stared at him. "You can't be serious. Me? Skinny, ugly, self-conscious, under-goaled, under-achiever? Me?"

He shook his head. "Didn't you ever look in a mirror?" He turned a corner. "Don't you ever now?"

She snorted. "Matter of fact, I meet that homely old woman face to face two or three times a day."

"There must be something wrong with your mirror. You should be seeing," he paused as he steered around another cramped corner, "an ageless and astonishingly beautiful woman who is full of life and energy and compassion and—." He grinned as he checked his rearview mirror. "You get the idea," he said.

"My gosh," Pat whispered, her cheeks even hotter.

Frank reached to press the radio button. "Relax," he said. "We have hours, and I want you to tell me more about Colin."

She said nothing for a few minutes, the Debussy melody filling the car with subtle comfort. "You know," she finally said, "I don't want to talk about Colin anymore. If you want me to, I'll write some more pieces for you to use in your book."

"Great. No more cruising Durbin? Anywhere else you'd like to stop on our way back?"

"There are so many—." She looked hard at him. "Did you know Mamie Arbogast?"

Frank shook his head. "Who was she?"

Pat giggled. "A woman who changed my life—or maybe did not change it. I'm not sure whether or not Patsy Yokum is still with me, one way or the other."

"What does that mean?" Frank asked.

Pat shook her head. "I'd rather see if she's still around. I forgot to ask Jessie."

"Want to go back?"

"No—let's go to Mrs. Arbogast's house if it's still there."

It was, weather beaten and gray, some of the shingles gone and the rest warped. All of the other houses on the dirt road had been abandoned, their windows boarded up, their yards decorated by scraggly weeds, but the door to the Arbogast house was open, and a car was parked on the sparse and dying grass. As she got out of Frank's car, Pat peeked into the window of the Cavalier, and she turned to Frank. "It's from a hospice," she said.

The person from the hospice was there, indeed, as were a middle-aged man and his wife. The man came to the door and, sour-faced and shabby, invited them in. "Who are you?" he asked.

"An old friend of Mrs. Arbogast's," Pat said. She smiled to put the man at ease. "And you are?"

"Son. Chauncey Arbogast," he said. "You can come in." He turned to point behind him. "My woman's in the kitchen."

Frank reached to shake Arbogast's hand, but his gesture was ignored.

"Could we see your mother?" Pat asked.

"She can't talk," Arbogast said. "Got Lou Gehrig's. Can't walk neither. That's how come Glorianna and me is here. Taking care of her." He led the way to the doorway of the back room. "Hospice woman's with her."

"We're both hospice volunteers," Pat said. She didn't explain further.

"Go on in," Arbogast said. He turned away.

The nurse's aide was gently bending Mamie's leg, then massaging the calf. Her fingers moved to the instep of Mamie's foot, and then she looked up. "I'm almost through," she said. To the old lady she said, "You've got company, sweetheart."

Pat was looking at Mamie Arbogast. The woman who had seemed old to her when Pat was young now looked ancient. Her face was deeply lined, her mouth slightly open, showing dentures. Her long white hair was in a neat braid down her back, and she was wearing a faded t-shirt that read "Feed My Sheep." Both hands lay in Mamie's lap, palms up, the long-nailed fingers permanently curled in atrophied positions. A blanket lay across Mamie's lap and down over her legs. She looked up and frowned.

"I'm Patsy Yokum," Pat said, "and it's very good to see you. My mama was Ruth Yokum. Do you remember the bed and breakfast lady?"

Mamie's eyes lit up, and she slowly nodded. "Uh," she said, "uh, uh."

The hospice aide explained. "Mrs. Arbogast has ALS. Do you know about it?"

Frank answered. "We're both with hospices."

"You're a nurse?" the woman asked Pat.

"Volunteers," she smiled. "Patient care and other things."

The woman picked up her tote bag. "I'm going to have to go, but I'm sure Mrs. Arbogast would like to have you stay a while"

Pat pulled a chair close to the old woman's recliner and sat down. Frank stood behind her. She leaned forward. "I was just telling my friend about you," she said. "We came back to town for a visit."

Mrs. Arbogast labored to nod.

"I've been living in Logan," Pat said, "and Frank lives in Pittsburgh. He's from Durbin, too."

Mrs. Arbogast nodded again. "Uh," she said as if understanding Pat's every word.

Pat picked up a frail hand. "Do you remember when you and Mama decided that I might make a good midwife like you, and you took me along on one of your visits?"

Mrs. Arbogast's lips twisted into a half-smile.

"You do," Pat said. "Well, I'm going to have to tell Frank about it. Would that be all right?"

Mrs. Arbogast nodded once more.

As she spoke, Pat gently rubbed Mamie's hand with both of hers. "I remember it was a rainy day, and I remember school was closed because the creek was flooding. Mama and I walked down to the grocery store, and she did her shopping, and then we met you at the post office and you asked if I wanted to go up the holler with you."

Turning her head with obvious pain, Mrs. Arbogast looked out the window and nodded toward the road. "Yes," Pat said. "You had an old Jeep, a really old Jeep, and the road to the cabin that you needed to visit was solid mud. We slid all over the place," Pat laughed.

Mrs. Arbogast smiled more widely.

"We crossed so many creeks and climbed so many hills that day that I couldn't count them," Pat said. "We finally got to a really shabby old cabin back up at the end of nowhere. An old man came to the door looking fearful, really scared, and he told us to hurry, hurry, hurry."

Mrs. Arbogast nodded and looked at Frank, apparently to make sure he was listening.

"The woman was lying on the floor in what was supposed to be a bedroom," Pat continued, dramatizing the story for Frank's benefit. "She was on a cornhusk mattress that rustled and crackled as she writhed around, and she looked like a grotesque balloon, like one of those that carnival people squeeze into all different shapes like dogs and clowns, but she was just all balloon in the middle with sticks for arms and legs. She was in hard labor."

Pat turned to look at Frank. "I can still hear her whispering, 'Help me, help me, help me.' I can still see her eyes, the pupils as distended as an old mine portal."

"What did you do?" Frank asked. He looked first at Pat and then at the old woman.

"Mrs. Arbogast started flinging out orders," Pat said. "Hot water, towels, rags, I can't remember what-all. But you know," she frowned, "the cabin was clean, just scrubbed and shining like it was some king's domain. And it smelled clean, like lanolin. I didn't see a scrap of food or extra clothes, but that cabin was clean."

"The woman gave birth?" Frank asked.

Pat stroked Mrs. Arbogast's hand. "With a lot of help from this wonderful lady."

A poor imitation of a chuckle came from Mamie.

"There were two babies, tiny, bloody twins," Pat said.

"Wonderful!" Frank said.

Pat shook her head. "They never even cried. In spite of all Mrs. Arbogast did and in spite of all the prayers I kept aiming at the ceiling, and in spite of the old man's tears and the woman's wailing, those babies were born dead." She turned to the Mamie Arbogast. "Wasn't the mother's name Rachel?"

Mrs. Arbogast shook her head.

"Ruth? Rebecca?"

Mrs. Arbogast nodded.

"Rebecca was about twenty years younger than the man," Pat said.

"What happened to the babies?" Frank asked.

Pat stretched her back and looked straight at him. "It had finally stopped raining, so I helped the man dig a hole in the backyard and put the cardboard carton in it while Mrs. Arbogast cleaned up Rebecca and the house. We shoveled the dirt back over the hole, and he marked the spot with a broken chair."

"A what?" Frank stared.

"He said he would mark it properly when he and the babies' mother could have a little funeral for them." Pat sighed. "We had to burn our clothes when we got home, right?" she asked the old woman.

Mamie's smile had vanished. She gave them a small nod.

"After you reported the deaths?" Frank said.

Pat shook her head and leaned close to the patient. "Can I tell him the rest of the story?" she asked.

The woman nodded, her eyes filling.

"I was wrong in thinking the man was the woman's husband." Pat took a deep breath. "He was her father—and the babies' father."

"My God," Frank breathed.

"Mama and Mrs. Arbogast went out and brought Rebecca to

town as soon as they could. They put her on a bus to go live with her brother and his family in Georgia. Mama told me that part years later."

Frank and Pat saw Mrs. Arbogast droop. Her eyes closed.

"We'd better go," Pat said. They stood, and Pat leaned to kiss the old woman's cheek. "You're a good woman, Mamie Arbogast. God bless you," she said. "We'll tell your son we're leaving."

Mamie's chin had dropped down onto her chest. She was asleep.

Chauncey just called "Yeah" from the kitchen. They never saw his wife. Pat watched Frank lay a fifty-dollar bill on the scarred coffee table.

"So," Frank said as he climbed back into his car, "you decided not to become a midwife. You got any other happy memories to share? Happier?"

"Lots," she said. Pat took a deep breath and reached to touch his hand. "I really want to go home," she said. "I'm about to have a panic attack."

He looked over at her. "Are you serious?"

She smiled weakly. "Not quite, but so much has been happening—so many memories, so much being churned up—I'm feeling so anxious that I want to get out and run for a hundred miles or else find a punching bag and give it thunder. I've missed my workout for two whole days. I'm about to explode."

"What can I do?"

"Drive like hell." She leaned back against the headrest. "Tell Carl Hess or whoever to play lullabies." She closed her eyes. Then her head came forward and she looked to her right. "No. Let's go down to the river."

"Any special spot?"

"The boat ramp," she suggested.

And there it was, the concrete slab that led to the last six or eight feet of mud. Willows branches, their leaves bright green, tickled the sun-flecked ripples, and as Pat and Frank walked down the cement, a frog leaped from the bank into the water. Four crows scolded the intruders, then flew to the other side of the river.

"A lot happened here," Frank said.

"Like eating lunch and being late back to school," Pat offered.

"And swimming until someone would come to tell us it wasn't allowed," Frank added.

"And fishing for fish that didn't exist, even when we were really little."

"I read somewhere that the river has been cleaned up," Frank said. "They say there are sunnies and catfish now, a few bass. I remember Colin and me spending his days off here. Must not be much mountain-top removal around here yet."

"Yet," Pat said. "This is right where he was baptized. That's what I remember best of all."

"You want to talk about it?" Frank offered.

She waited a minute, then said, "I'll write about it."

"Good. How's the panic attack?"

"Lurking," Pat said as she took his hand. "Let's go home."

In the car, she leaned back again, and this time, with a Schubert sonata in the background, she fell asleep, waking again when Frank stopped for gas.

"Where are we?" she asked. Then she realized. "Flatwoods, of course. Times Square, West Virginia. If you sit here long enough, you'll see everyone you ever knew."

"And a few others," Frank said as he opened the door and got out. "There are some I never want to lay eyes on again. Like our first grade teacher. Remember her?" He closed the door and turned to the gas pump.

"Our first grade teacher," Pat said as they got back on I-79 South. "What about her?"

"You've read *The Dollmaker*," Frank said.

"Of course."

"Our first grade teacher was the woman Gertie Nevil had to fight with. Our Miss Thurman had come down into the hills from Massachusetts on some kind of a mission, probably to educate us ignorant hillbillies, and she sure wasn't any Christy. There wasn't any kindergarten back then, so most of us couldn't read yet, and she told us flat out that it was disgraceful, that we were nothing but red-necked turkeys. Hell, most of our parents had trouble reading themselves, let alone teach us. You and your mother and your brothers were the exception."

Pat laughed. "Not that it did my brothers much good, bucko."

"Anyhow," Frank said, "my folks figured that was what school was for—to teach us to read and write—so they hadn't bothered. But after my mother heard that Miss Thurman was calling us hoopies and rednecks and all, she came charging down to the school, and she said that she had heard that the teacher was putting all us dummies in the back row and sending us to the cloakroom if we whispered and wasn't letting us choose our own partners for games—Miss Thurman teamed up dummies with dummies—and she was giving us dummies only the stubs of crayons and giving the brand new ones that we had brought to the smart kids. My mother didn't pull any punches.

"What brought her to school that day," he continued, "was the fact that I had asked to go to the bathroom and Miss Thurman wouldn't let me, and I wet my pants and then she made me stand in front of the room in my wet pants for the entire rest of the day. Mama went to the principal and said she'd also go to the school board if that teacher's contract was renewed."

"Was it?" Pat asked. "I can't—"

"Miss Thurman had connections."

"Ah-ha! I never knew that. I still don't remember. That's the end of the story?"

"Not quite. As soon as Mom saw that woman's name in the paper as having been renewed, she called Charleston and they came up and cleaned out the whole closet—the principal and the teacher and half of the members of the Board of Education. Mom ended up being elected president of the PTA the next year. She had a one plank platform—Durbin did not need people like the above-mentioned teacher serving as role models for its children. Period." Frank pushed a button, and the radio went silent.

"She was right," Pat said. "I do remember her being big into school stuff."

"There were plenty of times after that when we egged Mom on

to fight for us with our teachers or coaches, but she never did again. She always told us that the two most important lessons we could ever learn were how to deal with difficult people and how to turn a bad job into a good one. School, she said, was a good place to learn those lessons."

"I remember that woman now, that Miss Thurman," Pat said. "Big-boned and dyed red hair. What ever became of her?"

"She was caught sleeping with the principal, so she went into politics."

"Frank!" Pat laughed. "Are you sure?"

"Absolutely. Your mom found out from a bed and breakfast friend of hers in Elkins that they had been up there together, so your mom told my mom, and that was another reason to call the state Board, and they came, and Miss T. went back to New Hampshire— no, Massachusetts. The principal ended up teaching math over in Ellenboro." Frank grinned at Pat. "Honey, Miss Thurman became Mrs. Oliver Hermann in New Hampshire, and she is currently a representative in their legislature."

"My gosh," Pat breathed. "And I thought I was the one and only Three Faces of Eve."

Frank surprised her by pulling off at a rest stop, but neither of them made a move to get out of the car. "How long has it been, Pat?"

She thought a moment. "Three years? It's been four since Colin's funeral, but you called a few times after that, and I'm sorry, I've been so busy—and I think I've changed a lot, sort of—," she paused, "—deteriorated."

"Honey," he said as he laid his hand on her leg, "you haven't changed a bit except for the better. You are still that girl I used to adore—and still do."

"You're embarrassing me," Pat said, her face hot again. "You've changed, Mr. O'Connell. You never used to lie. And," she said firmly, "you didn't used to be married."

"No lie," he said as he climbed out of the car to go to the bathroom. Pat followed suit. He handed her a cup of coffee when she returned to the car.

She set the cup into the beverage holder and then, turning in the seat, Pat reached for a book on the floor of the backseat. *Sitting Around on the Mountain* by Francis B.E. Zastro. "Is your book going to come out with a hard cover or a soft one?" she asked.

Frank laughed. "I haven't written it yet. If it's anywhere near good enough, I'll have to find a publisher, and I think it's the publisher who decides on the cover. What do you have in mind?"

"Colin," Pat said. "I suppose he was proud of me from time to time and from thing to thing, but there was once—kind of special—"

"Tell me," Frank said.

Pat frowned. "It was a long time ago. We had taken the kids and had gone to some kind of a fair. Petersburg or Moorefield. Anyhow, there were all kinds of booths and all the stores were open, and there was a whirly-gig ride for the kids." She refastened her seat belt and held the book so that Frank could see it. "This Zastro guy was there with a bunch of his books."

"Really?" Frank asked. "You met him?"

Pat snorted. "Yeah, so to speak. I saw this book, and I opened a copy of it and there were all kinds of directions for making interesting furniture, like spice cabinets and doll display cases."

"That's why I bought the book," Frank smiled. "I thought I might get into making some for a hospice bazaar or something."

"Well, there was this Zastro fellow, and there were the books, so I asked Colin if I could buy one, and he said of course, so, because we didn't have a whole lot of money back then, just barely more than enough to meet our basic needs, I picked up a paperback copy, and I asked politely—"

"Like always," Frank smiled.

"—If Mr. Zaztro would please autograph the book for me. I had already handed him the money." She turned the book over and looked closely at the bottom right corner. "It was $7.95 plus tax back then, as against about $25.00 for hard cover. I mean, he didn't have any reason to think I would have the book autographed and then not pay him."

Frank looked both ways before merging back onto I-79.

"He very firmly told me he autographed only the hard cover edition," Pat continued. "He said he would not autograph a paperback even for the President of the United States."

"He said that?" Frank said.

"Would I make it up?" Pat asked. "Do you know what I did?"

"I hope you told him to shove his book right up his—"

Pat laughed. "Not quite. I ever-so-politely looked Francis B. E. Zastro in the eye, laid his precious paperback book back down on the table, and said, 'Mr. Zastro, if I ever write a book, and if it is ever published in both hard and paper editions, and in light of the fact that not everyone in this world can afford twenty-five dollars for a book, I will autograph every single copy that is ever published.'"

"What did he say?"

"I wasn't finished. I told him that if the President of the United States asked me to, or anyone other than Mr. Francis B. E. Zastro asked me to, I would autograph a roll of toilet paper."

"You said that?"

"I did indeed, and then I told him I wanted my money back. I was so mad!"

"You got it."

"Colin was there, and his mouth was hanging open because he would not have bet so much as a two-penny nail on me speaking that way to anyone, let alone someone as important as Francis Zastro. And do you know what Colin did?"

"Bought the hard cover and had it autographed for you."

Pat looked over at him and noted his grin. "Not hardly," she said. "He told me to keep that money, and he gave me two ten dollar bills, all he had left in his wallet, and said I should spend it all any way I wanted to."

"And what did you spend it on?" Frank asked.

"We all had barbequed chicken and baked potatoes and lemonade, and I gave Colin back the ten dollars and seventeen cents left over, and he gave each of the kids three dollars and told them to buy something for Mama with it."

"Did they?"

She laughed. "Celia bought me a clown doll, and Rosella gave me a ten-cent windmill thing, one of those pinwheels on a stick?"

"And spent the rest on herself."

"Rides. The whirly-gig. Roswell ate about a dozen corndogs and brought me the sticks and said I could use them for caramel apples for Halloween."

"Did Colin know?"

Pat nodded. "Celia was the only one who got her weekly nickel allowance for about the next two months. Roswell threw a fit, as you might imagine. Rosella never said a word, just set her jaw and didn't speak to us for those two months. She's always been like that. So has Roswell." She was quiet for a moment. "Celia—"

Frank waited for a semi to go around them, and then he said, "Celia is sick."

"She is," Pat said. "I'm not." She lay back against the headrest. "Not any more," she added. Within moments, she was asleep.

When she woke again, they were in her driveway. Frank had gotten out of the car and was opening her door. He was taking her hand, and he was helping her up, and he was saying goodnight.

"Can't you stay?" Pat managed to think and say.

He looked up at the house. "Celia seems to be here and awake. Let's not get her agitated. I'll head back, stop somewhere on the way."

"I wish—maybe Celia would like having you here."

Frank smiled and pulled Pat to him. "Let's not risk it tonight. I'll be back."

"When? Do you know—thank you—"

He nodded as she pulled back. "It's been good for me, too, honey. More than good." As he walked her to the door, he said, "Tell you what. You write a few more pieces about Colin—or yourself—and I'll write some of the stuff I remember, and then we'll see what we have. I'll call you tomorrow—or the next day."

She reached to put her arms around Frank's neck, and she kissed him.

"Be careful," she said. She watched him drive away. Why in God's name—forgive me, God, she thought—had they not taken advantage of that lovely little room in Durbin?

Chapter 9

It was only 4:30 in the afternoon when Frank left. They had forgotten lunch, Pat realized, probably because of Jessie's excellent breakfast. While she was thinking of it, Pat decided, she would e-mail a few good recipes to the Delightful Durbin Bed & Breakfast. Herb bread, sweet potato pie, three-bean salad, plus her favorite recipe for leftover roast beef, a Hungarian casserole. Jessie would like that.

First, though, she should check on Celia. Pat climbed the stairs, humming a hymn under her breath, and knocked on Celia's door. No answer, but she heard noises. She knocked again. Still no answer, just more movement. "Are you okay?" Pat asked.

"Fine," Celia said, and her voice sounded clear, even happy. "Just reading, Mother."

"Okay," Pat said. "Let me know when you're hungry and we'll fix something."

There was a giggle from behind the door. "I won't be," Celia said.

Pat frowned, then reassured herself. Leave well enough alone, she decided.

"Okay," she said again. "I'll be downstairs."

She took a quick shower, pulled on jeans and a shirt and put her corduroys aside to be dry-cleaned, her two-day-old underclothes into the hamper in the bathroom. Even that made her smile. What a good time she and Frank had had! But it was time to get back into harness. What to do first?

The cats! Oh, Lord, when had she last fed them? She ran down to the basement, expecting mewing, wailing, gnashing of cat teeth. No cats. There was scattered litter box filler on the floor, but there were no litter boxes. No water dish. No food. No cats.

What had Celia done with them? She might have let the cats out, but she wouldn't have removed all the equipment. Pat sat down on the step and looked around once more. No cats. Then she realized. Roswell had been back. He and his wife—what was her name?—

had come back for their beloved cats. How had they gotten in? Of course! Roswell had the key she had loaned him. Would he come again? What would he want? Had Celia known about his visit?

As she pulled herself up, she whacked the wall with her open hand. "Oh, heck!" she said aloud. "Who cares?" At least the cats were gone.

In her studio she turned on the computer and sent Jessie four from-memory recipes plus the one for Hungarian Beef from her recipe file. "Thanks for a GREAT stay," she added. "The Double-D is not only Delightful but also Delectable and Divine, and so are you, Dear."

Then she leaned back and took a deep breath. Today had been—and still was—a good time to think about the old days, the days with Mama and Colin—and Fonzie O'Connell. She smiled. Which story should she write down? Colin's baptism. Her visit to Wales. The birth of their first child, Colin's beloved Celia. A trip to Kentucky. As the scenes popped into her head, Pat scribbled reminders onto a scrap of paper. How many could she write before Frank came back? Not many, she hoped. He would be back soon, she hoped.

Standing at the window, she watched the breeze rustle the trees across the road and behind Stephanie's and Dolly's houses, and she remembered one of her favorite stories about Colin. The first words came hard on the computer, and then the letters began to spill onto the page faster than she could type them.

> It happened every year, that fund-raiser for the Durbin clinic. As long as the kids were little, we didn't try to go back home for it, but one time we left them with Mama for the day, and Colin and I went riding.
>
> Now, I had grown up on a farm, and Colin had grown up in Wales, so we both knew how to get on a horse, but it had been a while. Fortunately, nobody cared—the others on the Horses for Health ride were no better off than we were.
>
> I remember the trail like yesterday. Up into the mountains above town, the trees all gold and red and yellow because it was September or October, and it was

cold enough that the horses were feeling frisky—and so were we.

They—the people running the thing—gave me a nice little chestnut mare. Various people had brought extra horses. There were bunches of trailers around when we got there.

So I had this little chestnut, and Colin had a big old Appaloosa named Pete, and there were about twenty other people and we had a wonderful time talking and laughing and even singing on the way up the mountain.

When we got as far as we were going to go, the guide had us all get off our horses and tether them, and she opened her saddlebags and pulled out thermoses of coffee and hot cider plus sandwiches and cookies, and we all sat around on rocks or the ground (like Colin) and talked about the WVU-Marshall football game the day before, and our kids and where we had ridden horses before.

There was this one couple that had gone on riding tours in the British Isles, even Wales! Their name was Tompkins, and the man's grandfather had immigrated to the US, or rather to Halifax, Nova Scotia, where he worked as a cook on the big fishing boats. He was also a barber, I think, because the man said he remembered when his grandfather got old, he lived with them and he had a little barber business in the basement of their house.

That man and Colin had a lot to talk about! While they talked, I went for a walk in the woods with a nurse from the clinic, and she told me about some of the patients they had had lately, and I told her about Mamie Arbogast and maybe being a midwife and stuff like that.

Things got really exciting on the way back. Going uphill is a lot easier for horses than downhill, and the trail was pretty rocky and the horses slipped a lot, and one of them slipped so hard that he went down on his knees, and the man riding fell off and got his leg broken. At least that's what the nurse said, and he shouldn't ride the horse down, and it was getting toward dark because we had ridden a long way, so at first nobody knew what to do about him. My Colin did, though. He said, "I'll stay here with him. Leave us your coffee and my horse, just in case, and send an emergency crew up here."

The nurse offered to stay, too, but the man said he was just hurt, not dying, so she didn't have to. I felt really funny leaving Colin up there on the mountain, and I offered to stay, too, but he said no, that I had to get back to the kids. He said he would ride back into town on the ambulance or whatever they brought.

He didn't. It was way after dark by the time the police (that's who came) got the man down off the mountain, and they didn't have room for Colin, so he had to ride that horse all the way back to town. Remember, it was pitch dark, and all he had was one police flashlight which went out, he said, when he was only about half-way home, and he had to let the horse feel his way from there because it had clouded up and had started raining, and believe me, I got worried because he didn't come and didn't come and didn't come, but finally he did.

I can't remember what became of the man, but—.

Pat was in the middle of that sentence when the phone rang. She picked it up on the first ring, almost expecting Colin's voice. Instead, it was Jerry's. "Hey, you lady," he said, "you finally home?" He had, he said, called the night before and again this morning, but "Your daughter, she not know where you are. I kinda worried, Mrs. Patsy."

Looking out the window toward Jerry's empty house, Pat said, "We decided after church yesterday to drive up to Durbin, my hometown."

"Your Celia and you."

She hesitated. "No. A friend of mine who is also from Durbin. I hadn't been there in years. Oh, Jerry," her excitement rose, "I wish you had been with us. Our old bed and breakfast is run by a really nice woman, and we went to see an old midwife and we saw the river where I was baptized and Colin was baptized and it was good to go back." She laughed. "But I'm glad I'm not running that B & B anymore."

"Me, too," Jerry said. "Otherwise I never meet you. I am missing you, my lady friend."

"I miss you, too, Jerry," Pat said. She giggled. "And I miss our patio parties. Your wine is so good!"

He laughed loudly. "Now you drinking that Falling Tree stuff? I think I better hop on plane and bring you good stuff." There was a moment of silence. "Oh, my goodness, Patsy lady."

"What?" Pat asked.

"The good stuff still in my basement."

She paused, remembering the rich, grapey flavor of his homemade wine. She remembered, too, a very special bottle he had brought back from Europe and had saved for years, he said, for a special occasion. That occasion had happened on Patricia Tazewell's back patio when the moon was full and the air was warm and Jerry, he had said, was celebrating with his neighbor who was also, he had said, a very accomplished artist. It had, indeed, been a special occasion, a moment when Pat had herself felt special. That was the night when she had told Jerry about Colin and about Celia's problems and about her two ungrateful children who lived in Boston and New Mexico, and he had told her about bringing Tiffany to live near very nice neighbors so that she could be nice herself and yes, Jerry had always made Pat feel special. He had kissed her that night, her first kiss since Colin. She had worried about Tiffany, but not very much and not for very long.

"You mean you forgot to take your wine?" Pat now asked.

"Me and the boys, we leave in such hurry—that good stuff is still in cellar. You, Pat," he said. "You go over, get wine before new people come. You take to your house I am thinking."

"What a shame!" Pat said. "Do you want me to send it to you?"

He laughed. "Put stamps on?"

She laughed in return. "I could get a crate and ship them," she said.

"No shipping," Jerry said. "Colorado got good grapes. I make more soon. You keep them. Souvenir of Jerry."

"I'll keep them for you," Pat said. "You can come get them and the empties I was already saving for you."

She could hear him smiling. "You bring them to Steamboat Springs."

"In my suitcase," she giggled.

"Suitcase, hands, no matter. Or leave them in closet. No matter about wine. You come."

She thought hard for a moment. "You really want me to?"

He took so deep a breath that she could hear it. "Soon?" he asked.

"Not tomorrow," Pat said.

"Next day?" Jerry asked.

"Not quite," she smiled.

"You will like Steamboat Springs, Colorado. I got snowshoes now, too."

He asked about Celia. She told him about Roswell. She told him more about Durbin. They talked for almost an hour.

After he hung up, Pat wondered why she had not mentioned Frank. Or the book they would be working on together. She sighed, then finished writing her story.

Colin got home finally, and he took a hot shower and we went to bed—together—but he never even caught a cold, and the way he talked about that adventure later, you would have thought we had just trotted around the park a few times in the middle of the day with plenty to eat and a flashlight that didn't go out.

This story is important because it tells a lot about how Colin was, but also about what it was like to be married to such a man. He was, I think, proud of me from time to time and maybe a little bit a lot of the time, but I was proud to be his wife every minute I ever knew him. It was awesome to be able to say, "I am Mrs. Colin Tazewell, the wife of that man who—" and I always had plenty of stories to tell, including our Horses for Health ride up that mountain.

There was the sound of movement upstairs, and Pat got up and went on into the kitchen to fix some supper for herself and Celia, and, sure enough, there on the table was her spare door key. She took a deep breath and let it out. At least Roswell would have to knock if—when—he came back.

She dropped the key into a drawer, then pulled from the refrigerator a block of sharp cheddar cheese and a loaf of seven-grain bread. A grilled cheese sandwich—tons of cholesterol and megatons of calories, but she had skipped lunch, and she loved grilled cheese sandwiches, and she was hungry. Celia liked grilled cheese, too. Salad. Leftover spice cake.

She turned when she heard footsteps on the stairs. Too heavy for Celia, she realized, and when she turned, there was Walker. Her mouth open, she stared. "Good evening," he smiled.

Behind him, Celia was barefoot, wearing shorts and a t-shirt with no bra. Smiling sweetly, she echoed Walker's words, "Good evening, Mother. We're hungry."

Somehow, Pat managed to slice the cheese and butter the bread and heat the griddle and toss a salad and find in the freezer some ice cream and brownies she had baked and had been saving for the new neighbors. Celia set the table while Walker cleaned up the clutter of Sunday papers and empty pop cans in the living room. He even knew where the recycling bins were in the garage, Pat realized.

"Were you here," she asked, "when Roswell came for his cats?"

Celia frowned. "Is that what the noise was? We—I—heard someone downstairs, but I thought it was you. It was Roswell? Is he still here?"

Pat smiled and shook her head. "No—he and his cats, human and otherwise, are, I assume, far gone."

They had just started eating, Pat chattering about Durbin and church the day before and Jerry's call and the price of cheese these days, when the noise began in Pat's backyard. "No!" she said, leaping up, knocking her chair to the floor behind her. "Those boys!"

This time there were at least a dozen of them. This time, instead of cleaning up the mess they had made two days ago and which Pat had forgotten about, they were scattering the debris far and wide, bringing more from the woods. Pat ran out onto the patio, shouting at the boys, flailing her arms as if to scare off crows. They looked like crows, in fact, all of them wearing dark, baggy jeans, oversized yellow and orange sneakers, black long-sleeved t-shirts with some kind of a logo on the front. They looked like a dozen clones of two originals. One group sported spiked black hair. The other group was smaller in both size and number and had brilliant blond hair, also dyed and also spiked.

Celia and Walker had come out behind Pat, and it was Celia who said, "My god, they're a gang, a California gang in Tremont City." She started to laugh, a nasty, out-of-control laugh that sent daggers through Pat's stomach. "Oh, Mother, this is wonderful. Your yard is being mugged." Then she was dead-sober and heading for the yard. "If you don't do something, my indolent Mother, I will, and it will not be pretty."

"Stop it, Celia!" Walker commanded, trying to hold her arm.

Celia, however, broke away. She rushed on out, hitting the closest boy, shrieking names at him, grabbing his spiked hair. That boy was reinforced by four others. They had Celia surrounded, and they were pounding on her, punching her in the stomach, pulling her beautiful hair, kicking her, stomping on her bare feet. Walker was out there with her, and he, too, was surrounded by mad dogs, snarling beasts, teenaged boys gone wild.

Pat, her breath coming hard, stumbled back into the house and grabbed the phone and punched in 911. "Hurry!" she said. "It's an emergency. Somebody is going to get killed. Hurry!"

She hung up, the screaming and shouting so loud now that her ears rang. A boy, his face like a gargoyle, was coming toward the house, and he was carrying a tree limb, and he was swinging it. Walker was grabbing him from behind, grasping the limb, pulling the boy right off his feet, swinging the limb and the boy until the limb flew one way, the boy another, propelled into the backs and sides and bellies of three or four other boys, and all of them—three or four or a dozen, it seemed—fell to the ground in a heap. Celia was on the ground, too, and two boys were pounding on her, but, teeth-bared and face bloody, Celia had hold of the leg of one of the boys, and he was falling on top of her, and the other boy was kicking not Celia but his buddy. Celia's t-shirt was torn, her right breast exposed and badly scratched.

Pat was out there, too, pulling boys apart, grasping at shirts, belts, hair. She was gasping for air, sweat running down her face, her back. And then she was on the ground, and she was being stepped on, held down, and when she managed to turn onto her side, she looked up, and it was Tom Faurault whose shoe was in the middle of her back, Tom Faurault was spitting on Celia lying there next to Pat. Tom Faurault was shouting, "You bitch! You crazy, lunatic bitch! They're going to lock you up. They ought to send you to the electric chair. You are crazy! You are crazy!"

And then Walker was pulling at Tom, and Walker was big and strong, even stronger than Tom, and Tom was shouting, "Who the hell do you think you are?" and he was falling on top of Celia, and Celia was screaming, and a police car was screaming, and police were coming from all directions. Boys were running into the woods, and Pat was turning her face right into the ground, and she was sobbing and sobbing and she realized that her pants were wet not with blood but with urine, but she didn't even know whether it belonged to her or to one of those monsters who had invaded her world, who had hurt her baby, who had destroyed and destroyed and destroyed.

And then, as someone lifted her—it was one of the police officers—she heard Tom Faurault's voice again. "They started it," he was shouting. "They called my boys names. They attacked my boys with weapons. These women are crazy. They ought to be locked up. They ought to be arrested." Two of the police were holding Tom

Faurault by the arms. Walker was kneeling over Celia. Pat heard herself sobbing, "Celia, Celia," and she saw Walker look up at her, and she heard Walker saying, "She'll be okay, Mrs. Tazewell. She'll be okay" The police officer was leading Pat to the swing that had been so warm with Frank sitting on it, and the officer was setting her down, and he was telling her to stay there, and she wondered where in the world of God and the angels she could possibly have gone anyway, and she was praying for Celia and for Walker and for the police officers and for Chloe, oh, poor Chloe with those monsters eating her food and sleeping in her house and breathing down her neck and the neck of that poor, sick, helpless baby. Oh, poor Chloe!

Finally, two policemen had taken Tom Faurault to their car, and they were taking him to the police station, and two other officers were talking to Walker, and then they were talking to Pat, and Dolly and Stephanie and Jack had come and were talking, too, and Pat heard Stephanie saying, "The oldest boy may be suffering from Attention Deficit Disorder." Oh, Stephanie, Pat thought. "Or perhaps even Tourette's Syndrome," Stephanie was saying. "He has a filthy mouth, and he is definitely the ring leader." At least that part was true, Pat thought. "The younger one seems normal," Stephanie was saying. Not for long, Pat thought. Not for long, not with that brother, that father.

"Where is Celia?" Pat heard herself ask. "Where is Celia?"

Someone was telling her that Walker had taken Celia inside and Celia was okay but was badly bruised and should see a doctor and Tom Faurault complained to the police about Pat and Celia, and then Pat was laughing, and she was crying, and she was missing Colin so badly she could taste it. Colin. Or Jerry. Or Frank. Or God. Oh, yes, God. And then Stephanie and Dolly and Jack and someone else were helping her into the house and into the bathroom next to her studio because Celia and Walker were in the bathroom upstairs. Walker in her bathroom? Walker in Celia's room?

Pat felt herself nodding. Yes, she was okay. The upstairs bathroom was free now, someone was saying. Yes, she could make it up the stairs with Stephanie ahead of her and Dolly behind. They led her into the bathroom. They turned on the shower. They handed her the shampoo. Stephanie helped her take off her clothes and get under the water, and oh, it felt good. It felt good.

Jack would go with her to the police station to make a statement, Stephanie said, and at the station a blue-shirted man and a blue-shirted woman listened to her tell about the boys and the mess in the backyard and the brown bags they had been carrying in and out of their basement door and the ganging up on her and Celia and Celia's Bipolar Disorder and yes, Celia sometimes yelled at them and at her and at herself, but she was never ever violent and had never hit anyone else that her mother knew about. She was going to a doctor and taking her medicine and Celia was really a good girl. What about those boys plus Tom Faurault stepping on her and spitting on Celia and Tom not blaming his boys for one single thing? The police would take care of that, they said.

Oh, Colin, Pat thought as she sat silent on the way back home. How much of me you took with you! How much of me is trying to find a way back! Did you send Fonzie? I wish you knew Jerry. Maybe you do. Maybe you arranged for him, too. But why didn't you warn me about Jamie? Is your Patsy Yokum still around, Colin? Who is this new woman, this woman who is pretending to be a stained glass artist? Why does it have to be so hard?

Somehow they got back to Blooming Rose Court, and somehow she got into the house, and yes, Walker had taken Celia to the emergency room and they were back already and Celia had no bones broken but had taken her medicine and had gone to bed. Walker was waiting to find out about the police station, and Jack was sitting at the table in Patricia Tazewell's yellow kitchen and was drinking coffee that Walker—what was his last name?—had made and so was Patricia Tazewell, who was listening to Jack Morrison tell Walker that the complaint against Pat and Celia had been dismissed. Chloe and Tom Faurault were being cited for child neglect and disturbance of the peace. Tom was being charged with assault and battery. The boys might go to juvenile detention or foster care or something or other. The Fauraults were being ordered to pay for the clean-up and repair of the Tazewell yard and the police were going to check out the gang business and the brown bag business and—oh, poor Chloe!

And then Walker and Jack were gone, and Colin was back in Pat's head, and Pat was in her studio, looking out at the houses with lights in some of the windows, and she was turning on her computer and she was sitting down to write about him and how he had confronted a monster.

We had to visit a mine, Colin did, and it was in eastern Kentucky in someplace called Dailey or Dunbar or something and we got through visiting the mine and were on our way back to Ashland, I think it was, and there was an ice cream stand by the side of the road. Someone was selling furniture along the road, too, and we stopped and I bought an old rocking chair for forty dollars that just barely fit in the back seat of the car. It turned out to be solid cherry after I refinished it and made a new seat for it and it is in our living room at this very moment and is probably worth over a hundred dollars but I paid only forty for it. We decided to have an ice cream cone, soft like Dairy Queen, which is my favorite, we walked over to the ice cream stand and up to the window to order our ice cream cones and there was this biker who was just sitting there straddling his motorcycle and flirting with the girl at the window. He looked at us and then at our car, and he climbed off of his motorcycle and stood up in his great big greasy boots. He took great big steps and thrust his dirty face with its long stringy hair and filthy beard right up into Colin's clean face and snarled at him just like a dog would. SNARLED and his breath reeked of moonshine or whatever and cheap cigarettes, and the girl was giggling at the window and this monster said, real low down, "You all best crawl back into that there West Virginia vehicle and crawl back to that shithole West Virginia. You ain't wanted here."

I took hold of Colin's arm and said I didn't want any ice cream after all, but Colin said, "Yes, we do," and the man who was really, really big reached down without even bending, like an ape does, and pulled a knife out of his boot and laid it up against Colin's nose.

Then Colin said, "Right, mate. No harm intended—until now," at which point Colin brought his knee up in exactly the right location and his fist into another right location (the man's fat belly), and the man crumpled into a big fat ball on the ground and Colin wiped his hands on a napkin he told the not-giggling girl to hand him, and she made the ice cream cones for us, and Colin paid for them and then put them right back in the girl's window. He got back in the car and came back to West Virginia, which is not a shithole, but not until Colin reported the man to the police so that the next time that monster attacks anyone whether from West Virginia or not, he will be locked up. But that's how Colin was, and that's why I don't know who I am anymore without him. I wish he was still here. He would take care of that Tom Faurault.

As she reread it, the piece sounded terrible. She would have to rewrite it before she could show it to Frank.

Frank. Pat picked up the phone, looked at the number scribbled on the notepad, and pressed the eleven numbers. She heard the ringing once, twice, three times, four. Then a metallic voice came on. It was Nancy's. "You have reached the O'Connell residence. Please leave your name and number and we will return your call as soon as possible." Of course. Frank couldn't have gotten to Pittsburgh yet. Pat smiled painfully, hoping that he had not stopped for any ice cream cones. But he could deal with monsters, too.

Jerry? He would tell jokes and serve wine and pretty soon everybody would be hugging everybody else. Either that or he would simply "knock blocks off the heads." No monsters lasted long in Jerry's world. Not even Tiffany.

Pat sighed. Her bed would feel good. Before she went upstairs, she looked at each house in the neighborhood, imagining who and what was behind each lighted window, and she sighed as she turned toward Jerry's dark house, and she said three quick prayers for the people in the lighted houses, plus one for Steamboat Jerry and one for Frank. Should she say one for Jamie? Of course she should, but she didn't.

She made the rounds to be sure that all of the doors and windows were locked, and she checked the sensor light on the back patio. It still worked. She went upstairs to check on Celia and to go to bed.

Chapter 10

Celia was still asleep when Pat woke the next morning, and Colin was still on Pat's mind. She thought of him lying in bed next to her, reaching for her, teasing her with a tickling finger across her chest, the fingers of his other hand tiptoeing across her legs, up onto her stomach under the sheet. She came awake suddenly. The fingers were not Colin's. It wasn't Colin at all. She threw the sheet back and leaped out of bed. A bat! It flew, bumped against the window, swooped back across the room, back over Pat's head, and fastened itself onto a drape. Pat put her hand to her throat. How the hell had that bat gotten in? What was she supposed to do with it? As cuddly as the conservationists might consider this ugly creature, it did not belong in her bedroom. How had Colin gotten rid of the bats in that old trailer, their very first home? Lights. He had turned on lights behind the bats, and they had flown to the darkness, eventually out into the night sky.

But it was now daylight, and Colin was not here.

The bat flew again, dive-bombing, gliding, flapping madly to find an opening to the outdoors, away from the world where it did not belong, out into the world where it did. Should Pat try to get the screen off, try to shoo the bat toward the open window? But that's where the bat was stationed—on the drape right next to the window— and the screens were hard to move.

Pat opened her bedroom door and slid out, closing the door behind her. She retrieved a towel from the hamper in the bathroom, then sneaked back into her room. This would work. But although she was able to cover the bat with the towel, she couldn't grasp it inside the towel. It got away, flying right past her head, the nest of her hair, the hem of her pajama top. It swooped to skim the arch of her foot, then landed on the carpet. Yes! Pat grabbed for the wastebasket next to her dresser, scattering its contents as she flipped it upside down and onto the bat. "Come on, you rascal," she whispered, "come on, try to get away. Fly up." It did not.

Pat reached backward for the towel, thinking she would engulf the bat while it lay on the floor. She tipped the edge of the wastebasket, and the bat came crawling right out at her. "No!" she whimpered, scooting the basket and again trapping the bat. How ugly that thing was up close! Those beady eyes, that nose, those ears. God, Pat thought, is this some kind of a joke? It's not funny.

Her shoes. She reached and put them on the top of the wastebasket. Then she ran out of the room, down the stairs, down to the basement where she found Colin's fishing net. But that wouldn't work. The holes were too big. Butterfly net? They had never had one. Bee bonnet? Hardly.

Back up to the kitchen. The colander. No, a sieve. She opened the drawer under the stove and grabbed one. She ran back upstairs, hoping against hope the bat would not have crawled out from under the wastebasket.

It hadn't. She pulled off her pajama trousers just in case the bat decided to get up inside them, and, bare-bottomed, she squatted and tipped the edge of the basket. There he was, turned away from her, in a clear space on her lovely, thick carpet. Hand shaking, she reached in and laid the sieve over the bat. Then she dragged the sieve toward her, onto the towel still lying on the floor. As if the bat had surrendered and was waving a white flag in his tiny claws, it lay perfectly still while Pat bundled up the sieve, the bat, and the towel. Still without pants, she crept out of the room and down the stairs and to the patio door. One-handed, she unlocked it, pulled it open, and threw bat, towel, and sieve onto the patio. She closed the door, leaned hard against it, and took a deep, deep breath.

As she filled the coffee pot with water, she began to laugh. Then she was laughing hard. Hysterical, no less. "Oh, Colin," she choked, "I did it. One little bat. One creepy little bat. But I did it."

Celia spoke from behind her. "In God's name, Mother, what in the hell are you doing? Who are you talking to? Where are your clothes?" She herself was wearing only a bra and bikini underpants—plus high-heeled sandals. Bruises showed on her arms, one leg, her face. Pat's heart skipped a beat. Another bad scene? From the tone of Celia's voice, it would be a low.

"Pill time?" Pat asked.

"I'll take care of the pills," Celia snapped. "You take care of your obscene appearance."

Pat bit her tongue to keep from saying, "And you take care of yours." Instead, she prayed as she climbed the stairs. Keep your hand on my mouth, Lord.

When she came back down, Celia had disappeared. Surely not outside. Pat looked at the patio. No Celia, and the sieve and towel were right where she had tossed them. Then she heard the shower turn on, and she breathed a sigh of relief. "Colin," she whispered, "you should not have left me with this." There was half a glass of water and a medicine bottle on the counter. Good. Celia had taken her medicine.

Pat read the morning paper while the coffee brewed. Then she took two cookies from the snack drawer and picked up her cup and went to her studio. Through the window she could see Jack Morrison backing his Lexus out of the garage, heading for his "filling station." There was no sign of life at the Faurault house, and, wonder of wonders, there was no sound of a baby crying.

It was Monday. Surely it was time for the boys to be up and getting ready for school, but that was none of her business. Maybe they were already in foster care—or jail. She must run over later to be sure there were no hard feelings between her and Chloe. Hopefully, Tom would be far gone, hopefully to work so that he wouldn't get fired for excessive absenteeism. Probably, however, he would be on his way to another of his stupid marathons. Too bad he had not gotten the boys into running. They could sweat off some of that disgusting behavior.

While she watched, a strange car pulled up in front of Dolly's house. Two men climbed out. Pat smiled to herself, remembering the hot summer night when she and Celia had been sitting on the front steps and had seen strangers approaching the Peters house. Dolly and Walker had lived there only a few weeks, pleased with the stained glass crescents that made up the panels next to her front door, the rain-forest scenes ornamenting the French door leading to her backyard, all of it ordered by telephone from Dolly's former home in

Illinois. She had been thrilled, and she had paid in full, and Pat had proved that she, a fine stained glass artist, was also honest and reliable and extremely talented. Pat had proved that to herself, too. She had even considered calling the local newspaper to come take pictures of all of the beautiful stained glass on Blooming Rose Court. That would be nice for the reputation of the whole development, she had thought, and she could mention the courthouse in Summersville and the church in Marlinton. Every little bit would help when it came to business.

But on this particular night, Celia and Pat had been sitting on the front steps, and Celia had commented on the fact that Dolly seemed to be much older than Walker. "Do you think they're really married?" she had asked Pat. "And what about that old Buick that was parked behind their house yesterday? Walker drives a green Taurus, and Dolly has a Chevy van. Neither of those cars is in the garage."

"It's none of our business, honey," Pat had said. "How do you know?"

"I walked by earlier," Celia said. "They have all brand new furniture. She's not from around here. What does she do, anyway? What does that Walker do?"

"I don't know, but they pay their bills," Pat had said. She had not told Celia that Dolly had paid her glass bill in cash and that she had heard that Dolly paid for her house, the total house, with a cashier's check. The source of anyone's income was a matter for Poirot or Columbo, not Celia and Patricia Tazewell.

It was then that another strange car had appeared and two men climbed out. "That's not Walker," Celia had said. "He's taller and has more hair."

"I have no idea," Pat said. "Maybe a pizza delivery man."

"There's no sign on the top of the car," Celia noted. "Can they see us?"

It was unlikely. Because of the bugs, Pat had not turned on the porch light. They watched as the men went up to the house and peered in the front window. Then they came down off Dolly's porch and crept around the side of the house and apparently into the backyard, and that was when Celia decided to call the police.

Pat chuckled now, remembering the embarrassment and how handsome one of the officers was and how she, Pat, had wished he would show some interest in Celia. The police had arrived after the men left, but Celia, using the flashlight from the glove compartment of Pat's car, had crept across the street and had written down their license plate number.

By the time the police arrived, Dolly was back home and had explained that the men were clients of hers. "Clients?" Celia asked the officer as he came back from Dolly's house. "What kind of clients? Was she expecting them?"

"I didn't ask, ma'am," the handsome officer said. "The lady just said they were okay. You ever have unexpected company?"

The tone of his voice had made Celia mad. "Unexpected company, yes, clients, no," she said. "And you need a change of attitude, mister." The other officer laughed and they left with Pat still wondering what it would be like to have a son-in-law on the police force. And when Pat sent an e-mail to Dr. Baltry describing the incident, he had told her that she had done the right thing, both in calling the police and in letting Celia take leadership in the affair. "Your most important role," he had e-mailed back, "is to be supportive and to listen and to let Celia take control of her own life." Easy for him to say, Pat thought. She had gone over the next day with a plate of brownies and apologized to Dolly. She politely, of course, tried to find out what "client" meant, but Dolly had not responded favorably. Not then.

Pat was still chuckling about that weeks-ago incident when she turned back to her computer. "Colin," she said aloud, "I hope you are enjoying all this, your stupid wife, your erratic daughter, your ignorant son and negligent other daughter." She sobered. "Oh, sweetheart," she whispered. "I'm sorry. I still miss you so much!"

That was what she decided to do. She would write another piece about Colin. Her glass work could wait.

Then the phone rang. It was, of course, Frank. "Just checking," he said. "Are you writing?"

"You're reading my mind again," Pat said. "I just turned on the computer. How's Nancy?"

"Talk to you again in a day or two," was all Frank said.

Reminded of the trip to Durbin, the football field, Mrs. Arbogast, the river, Pat began writing again.

Colin Tazewell was my very first love except for Bobby McIntire in the first and second grades and then again in seventh grade. (He is probably dead by now.) Warren Abelmier came in between, and then Billy Mahoney, Sr., the father of that Billy Mahoney who ruined our Rosella. Billy was captain and quarterback for the football team, so it is no wonder that all the girls including me were in love with him. He never paid any attention to me in spite of the fact that I was a cheerleader and track star.

But those loves don't count, not compared with Colin. He was very handsome in that beautiful Welsh way— dark-haired and small but very strong and with eyes almost as blue as the chicory that grows along the road. He twinkled. Maybe that's why I thought of sprites and elves for P.J.'s windows, to remind me of my real love. Colin was springtime, even when things were bad in the mines. And he had that Welsh accent. Most people thought it was English, but I corrected them.

Colin was a storyteller, like legends from his homeland and spooky stories about Druids and funny, funny stories about his family, especially his grandmother, who claimed to be of Druid descent. My Catholic friends when I was growing up always said that Druids were not acceptable in Christian circles and it was a sin even to think about them, but everybody with any sense knows that Druids were sort of mystics with a little superstition thrown in. Colin always smiled when I said that, like he knew something I didn't. Colin could handle Druids.

Anyhow, Colin was raised Catholic but had stopped listening to the priests before he ever came to Durbin. He always said he did not believe priests are any more saintly than coal miners—most of them—and that he, Colin Tazewell, could talk to God whenever he wanted, especially when he was underground, where the priest never was. He did not need any old man in a black dress to talk for him, he said.

Colin's original religion did not bother me, but it bothered my mother, and she talked to him about how he should be in favor of some religion and not just against Catholic, and Colin liked my mother a lot so he listened and said if she wanted to pray for him, it would be okay, so she did, and sure enough, before we got married and moved to Logan, Colin decided to be baptized by immersion, the real and original way.

So our minister at the Freewill church—I wish I could remember his name—announced there would be a baptism on such and such a date and anyone interested should contact him. Most of the people in Durbin were already baptized by one means or another, so Colin was the only one that particular day, and it was a good thing because it was very cold and windy, and anyone with a less sturdy constitution would have been down sick soon thereafter. The minister was.

Now, I had been baptized when I was nine years old, which is when most Baptist kids get baptized because that's when they have baptism classes in Sunday School, and when I was nine was when Mama decided that my brothers should be baptized. They had missed the baptism class when they were nine because that was the period when we had to take care of Grandma every Sunday while Grandpa went to church. So, baptism class or no baptism class, I decided that anything my brothers could do, I could do, too. So all three of us were baptized on the very same day, which was warm and sunny and the river was not flooding as it usually did that time of year. It must have been April, around Easter, a good time for baptisms.

That particular baptism didn't do much good for any of the three of us, my brothers turning out to be ungrateful and absentee sons and the baptism that really worked for me was Colin's. I was nearly adult at the time, adult enough to be getting married, and so was Colin, and here he was, an adult male in a town of good-old-boys who wouldn't be seen dead in church unless they were actually dead, and he was willing to stand up and be baptized. He put on his white shirt, and the minister had on his, and in front of God and nine-tenths of the congregation of the Freewill church, Colin and the minister marched down to the river bank and into that cold and windy water and I remember it all like it was yesterday because that was the day when I truly knew that I, too, had been saved. It didn't matter that I was shivering as I stood in the mud beside that river. It did not matter that we were singing "Just As I Am" off key and not very loud. It did not matter that I was going to have to wash and iron Colin's shirt again. He and I had both joined the ranks of the chosen.

That was when I knew that I deeply and truly and completely loved Colin and the Lord and still do.

Pat straightened up there on her chair in front of the computer, and she scrolled the copy back so that she could read it. As she corrected the spelling of "baptized" to have a "z" instead of an "s" and as she deleted a few surplus words, she wondered what Frank would think of this piece.

Yes, thanks to all these wonderful memories, plus the visit from Frank, she was, indeed, getting around to knowing who Patsy Yokum was—had been.

She had printed out and saved the copy and was turning to her stained glass projects when she heard the doorbell.

It was Jack Morrison. "Do you know anything about babies and fevers?" he asked.

She smiled. "I've been through a few," she said.

"Could you come over and look at Tracy?" he asked. "He's awfully hot, and he won't eat, and Stephanie has been up most of the night. I went and got some more baby Tylenol," he said, "but he won't take it." Jack looked sleepless himself; his sweat suit stained and stretched, his face unshaven, his eyes darkly circled.

"And you need to get to work," Pat said even as she flipped the switch on her front door so that it would not lock and followed Jack across the road.

Stephanie was waiting for them in the living room littered with blankets, a package of diapers, coffee cups, Stephanie's bathrobe. "I wish you'd called me sooner," Pat said as she laid her hand on Tracy's head. He was whimpering and restless, his eyes as dark-circled as his father's. "Poor little guy. Let me take him," she said, and Stephanie laid the baby in Pat's arms. "Maybe we ought to get him to the hospital," Pat suggested.

Stephanie shook her head. "I'm sure it's just a fever. Babies have them all the time." She sat down on the couch. For once, Pat noticed, her hair was not perfectly combed. She had on no make-up.

"How long ago did you try to give him the Tylenol?" Pat asked. She felt his forehead again. It was very hot and dry.

"Fifteen minutes," Jack said. He turned to Stephanie. "I've got to go," he said. "I have appointments."

Stephanie nodded, and he ran up the stairs, the sound of the shower coming soon after.

Rocking the baby, Pat walked the length of the large living room and then walked back. "He's awfully hot, honey," she said.

"I know," Stephanie agreed. "I don't know what's wrong."

"Has he eaten anything? Drunk anything? I think he's dehydrated."

"He can't keep anything down," Stephanie said. "He spit up the Tylenol."

"Let's try again," Pat suggested, and this time, Tracy, even with his eyes closed, did swallow and lick his lips. "We'll give him another in a half hour. If his temperature doesn't go down by then, I'll vote for the ER."

Downstairs again and clad in khakis and a dark, short-sleeved shirt, Jack leaned to kiss the baby's cheek and then his wife's. "It's hell being a dentist," he told Pat. "A real pain in the jaw." He tried to smile, but his worried eyes were on his son.

"You're a good dentist," Pat said. "Everybody says so. Unlike a few I've been to."

"Bad experiences are the ones we all hear about," Stephanie noted after Jack left.

"I'll bet you haven't heard any worse than some I could tell you," Pat said.

She lifted Tracy, hoping he would burp, but he just stiffened and whimpered, then let his head fall onto Pat's shoulder. "I wish I had inherited my father's teeth. He never had a cavity in his entire life." She chattered on. "I eat more candy than he ever did, though. I can't resist gum drops and jelly beans, especially Smuckers or Jelly Belly, and gum drops are just terrible for your teeth because they stick. If you absolutely have to eat candy, hard is best, I understand. And you should floss every day, right?" The baby's head felt hot even through Pat's sweatshirt. "I read recently," she said, "that flossing daily will lengthen your life by eight years. Now I ask you," she turned to Stephanie, "who in the world determined that? My bad dental experiences—maybe like Paul the Apostle said, I must be atoning for the sins of my forefathers. How else can you explain the excruciating agony of root canals?" She tried to laugh, but it came out a snort. "I guess I should be glad that it's my teeth and not my brain that is the problem."

"Do you want me to take him?" Stephanie asked. She was leaning back on the couch, her eyes closed.

Pat shook her head. She talked on, trying to divert Stephanie. "I guess the worst experience I ever had was right after Celia was born. It was in Logan, and that dentist is long since dead, thank the Good Lord—rest his soul. We had just moved and I had a terrible toothache, and Colin had to go to work, of course. So I took our Goodwill stroller and put Celia in it and walked about a mile to this dentist's office, the one the people in the next trailer had recommended—although I certainly don't know why. I got there and told the receptionist or whatever she was, about my toothache, and she said they had just had a cancellation and I could go on in and she would watch my baby." Pat looked over at Stephanie, who was asleep, her head at an uncomfortable angle. Walking to the back of the room and looking out at the woods, Pat continued anyway, bouncing Tracy gently. "That woman was very nice, but the dentist wasn't. When I went into the operating room or whatever you call it, there he was in the patient's chair, leaning back on the headrest with his mouth wide open so that I could see all of the thousands of fillings in his teeth, and he was snoring. He probably liked gum drops even better than I do. I said, 'Doctor?' and he woke right up. I remember he had oily gray hair, and his face looked like a coal miner's, all dirty in the crevices. His white coat was grubby and wrinkled, and he didn't even wash his hands before he pulled open my mouth and began poking around. I could only hope that the instruments were clean." She checked Tracy. No improvement, but he seemed no worse either. Maybe the drone of her voice was helping. "That idiot just kept looking at my teeth and saying, 'Hm-m-m, hm-m-m, hm-m-m.' I could hear Celia crying out in the waiting room, but he just kept saying, 'Hm-m-m.' Finally he said, 'New babies eat the enamel right off your teeth. Lots of work to be done here.'"

Stephanie was snoring lightly. Pat kept walking. "I asked him how much it would cost because we were really, really poor then, and he said, 'Three or four hundred. Payments if you want.' I could hardly keep from crying, but I said no, just fix the one that was hurting. No Novocain I said because I thought that would cost more. So he fixed it—a root canal with no Novocain if you can believe that. It still hurts just to talk about it."

Tracy began whimpering more loudly, and his belly was hard, his back rigid. Pat finished quickly. "And it turned out he fixed the wrong tooth, and I had to go to another dentist. Colin went to that creepy creep and told him he was going to sue, but of course we couldn't afford a lawyer, so we just didn't pay him. We had to pay the second dentist, though. He was better, but he was even more expensive and we had to pay him five dollars every two weeks, every payday. The first dentist was right about how much tooth trouble I would have, but you can bet we never went back to him." The baby was really crying.

"I'm sorry," Stephanie said as she stood and reached for Tracy. "Were you telling me something?"

Pat just said, "Nothing important."

"I'm going to try to put him down," Stephanie frowned, already heading upstairs. "Priscilla will be waking up. I'll call you if I need you, okay?"

Chapter 11

She went right to her studio and began cleaning tools, getting organized to cut some of the church glass. Having turned on the same Mozart CD she had been listening to when Ralph Sandusky stopped by, she was soon thinking about his visit, how reverently he had entered her studio, almost on tiptoe, almost as if he had been entering a sanctuary. "My word!" he had whispered as he glanced from the stacked finished panels to the sheets of glass waiting to be cut, to the bits of wire and scraps of color she had strung together and hung in the front window. "This is awesome," he said.

Surprised by his enthusiasm, Pat had guided a tour of the finished work, a clown, a snowman, a Bird of Paradise that she had put together simply on a whim.

Sandusky had reached a long finger to feel the surface of a piece of pebbled green cathedral glass that was lying on Pat's work table. He had moved close and stared at a sheet of bubbled brown glass. He had gently picked up a scrap of rosy-tinted clear glass and had held it up to the light, an imitation of the way she had later held a similar piece for Frank. Pat smiled. "I do that every once in a while myself just to keep a positive outlook on things."

"What are you working on now?" her pastor asked.

The next thing Pat knew, she was showing Sandusky how to push wet cement into the lead cames on a piece of a lampshade that she was repairing for a customer. She was guiding Sandusky's hands as he smoothed the edges of a piece of glass on the electric grinder. She was letting him pile sawdust on the piece he had cemented.

"We'll let that sit for a while," she explained, "so that it will absorb the oil from the cement. Then the sawdust gets brushed off and the cement gets pointed— trimmed— and then we turn the piece over and do the same thing on the other side."

He had stayed several hours, hardly talking, just asking questions, watching. Finally, after he had cleaned the cement and sawdust crumbs from his fingers and had put his jacket back on, he had left, but not before saying, "I'll never look at another piece of stained glass without remembering this delightful afternoon. Do you ever think of yourself as working hand-in-hand with the Almighty Creator? You do, you know."

Pat was smiling at that memory, her diamond-wheeled cutter moving exactly right along a piece of grape-colored glass, when the phone rang. It was Stephanie. The baby was worse. Could Pat ride with them to the emergency room and then drop Priscilla off at day care?

Of course, Pat agreed, checking to make sure all of her equipment was turned off or laid safely to the side. But when she went to get her car, it was gone. Celia had left with the Subaru. She called Stephanie back. Yes, they could take the Morrison car.

The baby was sick indeed. So was Priscilla. She had a temperature of 100.2 degrees, the Physician Assistant in the ER said, and should be in bed or at least playing quietly, definitely not endangering other children. No problem, Pat said. Priscilla could go home with her. Priscilla could help Grandma Pat, right?

They left Stephanie and Tracy at the hospital, Jack to come as soon as he could. On the way home, Pat stopped at Rite-Aid to get a supply of children's Tylenol and some ginger ale and a new box of crayons and a coloring book. She picked up a picture book she hadn't seen before, one with a delightful picture on the cover. *Cowboy Sam and Those Confounded Secrets*. Priscilla wasn't interested at the moment, but she would be. They would have a nice, quiet day, surrogate grandmother, surrogate granddaughter. And yes, Pat assured Priscilla, Tracy would be fine. He just needed a little extra caring for.

As they swung into the entrance to Blooming Rose Court, a car was coming out, and Pat barely missed it. It was a Grand Am with a Pennsylvania license plate. Frank! Again?

She pulled into the Morrisons' driveway. Frank turned around, and by the time Pat got Priscilla out of the Explorer and had pulled the packages from the back seat, Frank had parked and came across the road. His face was one big question. "Priscilla's not feeling very good," Pat said. "She's coming to my house."

He picked her up, Priscilla offering no protest but instead snuggling into his arms.

"You going to help your extra grandma today?" he asked, and Priscilla gave him a weak nod. "Me, too," he said. He turned to Pat. "Where's your car? I was afraid you had taken off for Boston or something."

"Celia has it," Pat said.

"Job?"

"Don't I wish."

Pat opened the door to let Frank and Priscilla in. "I thought you were going to call in a few days," Pat said. "You came back instead."

"You mind?" he asked.

"You know better," she said as she deposited the packages on the kitchen table. "Let me get Priscilla settled, and then we can talk. I've written only one more piece."

"That's more than I have."

She laughed. "You've been driving back and forth to Pittsburgh."

He shrugged. "I never got to Pittsburgh last night."

She washed her hands, then filled a glass with water and turned to him. "Where did you go?"

"Back to Durbin. I needed to find a little more of myself."

"I hope you found me, too," she said.

"Lots of clues," he said. "I'm almost there."

"Let me know when you find me," Pat said. She opened the drugstore package, pulled out the bottle of liquid Tylenol, and went into the living room where Frank had deposited Priscilla on the couch. The medicine went down with a feeble "Thank you." Priscilla lay back under the afghan Pat offered her, shook her head at the offer of the book, then asked, "Can I watch Ninja Turtles?"

Pat frowned to tease her. "No Ninja Turtles in this house, partner, but I think *Snow White* may be waiting for you." She pulled a cassette from under the TV set and slid it into the VCR. "Seven dwarfs, coming up," she said. "Don't try to sing along."

"Okay," Priscilla agreed.

Pat turned, almost bumping into Frank. "Good job," he said.

"Let's go to my studio," Pat said. "Unless you want a nap or something to eat."

"Nothing. I came to help."

"With what?"

"Whatever. Those trees you didn't know what to do with, your glass whatever. Whatever."

"Oh, my gosh!" Pat said, looking toward the garage. "I forgot all about Celia's trees. Are they still there? Those kids—" Then she realized that Frank hadn't been there for the backyard crime scene. "Have you seen Celia's trees?" she asked.

He frowned. "Not by name."

"Let's go look," Pat said.

"Hang on a minute," Frank said. He went to the kitchen and came back with a pot lid and a big spoon, both of which he handed to Priscilla. "Bang on this if you need anything," he told the little girl.

"You make a good grandfather," Pat smiled. She led him out the patio door into the yard.

"My god!" Frank stopped in his tracks. "What happened? Those boys again?"

Pat gestured toward the Faurault house. "Those boys again," she said. She went on around the side of the house and stopped. "That's what I was afraid of."

Celia's fragile ficus tree was on its side, most of its leaves gone, its branches broken. The ceramic pot was in pieces. The four saplings had been torn out of their plastic pots and had been strewn along the bank, their roots exposed. As they surveyed the destruction, Pat told Frank about the attack, about the police, about the citations.

"You want me to clean it up?" he asked. "A couple of hours—"

She shook her head. "I need to take pictures first. Evidence for the insurance company and the court."

"Got a camera?" he asked.

"Wait here."

He did. She returned. "I'll go in with Priscilla," she said, "if you'll take the pictures. I'm just glad Tom didn't think to clean it up."

"He'd better not. You could charge him on that count, too—destruction of evidence."

Pat could hear the phone ringing, so she hurried into the house. What next? she wondered. Thank goodness Frank had come back for her to bounce off of.

"Jessie?" Pat asked. "Jessie who?"

"At the B&B in Durbin—you stayed here."

"Of course. I had my feeble mind on a dozen other things."

"I wanted you to know that Billy John Yeager called me last night," Jessie said.

"Who?"

"Billy John Yeager. He said his name was Yeager. He's the man who told me about the Double-D being for sale."

Pat carried the cordless phone into the living room. Priscilla was asleep, and Snow White was busy cleaning the dwarfs' house. Pat leaned to touch her surrogate granddaughter's forehead. It was hot and dry. Oh, God, Pat prayed quickly. "Jessie," she said, "I'm in the middle—"

"I'll make it quick. This Billy John called, and I told him that the previous owner had stopped in a couple of nights ago, and he asked all kinds of questions about you. I didn't tell him your name or your address or anything, but I got to thinking about it afterwards and thought I ought to warn you or something."

A cold chill went through Pat's body. "What did you say his last name was?"

"Yeager. He still lives in Mars Hill. Would you like me to check up on him?"

"Not unless he gets in touch again." Priscilla was stirring, moaning in her sleep. "I have to go."

"Of course," Jessie said. "I'll let you know if I hear any more. Thanks for the recipes."

"Who's calling who?" Celia asked as she came through front door. "What the hell is going on here?"

Pat stared. There Celia stood, her satin shorts and top almost as skimpy as underwear. Pat felt sick to her stomach. Where had this ugly woman come from, her hair sticking out from her head, her eyelashes almost hidden by swollen lids. What had happened to the old Celia, that gentle, loving little girl of long ago? "I was trying to call you, Mother dear." She waved her cell phone. "You're always talking, talking, talking."

"I am not now," Pat said, trying very hard to stay calm. "Please get some clothes on. We have company."

Celia scanned the room, saw Priscilla on the couch, and laughed. "I wondered whether you had gotten so senile that you were watching cartoons. No—you're watching cartoons with that little crap from across the street. Don't you ever get tired of taking care of that she-nerd's kids?" She yawned and rolled her shoulders. "Is there anything to eat in this house? Since when is this—" she pointed, "—company? She practically lives here, my adorable little picked-up sister who is getting to be one big pain in the ass." She made a hideous face, came close to Priscilla, leaned down, and growled. "I'm going to eat you up!" she said.

Sound asleep, Priscilla did not move. Pat grabbed her daughter's arm. "Get away from her. Go get some clothes on. Frank O'Connell is here."

Celia slumped into the wing-back chair. "Oh, shit! That wuss from your childhood. That weeble that Daddy ran around with." She glared up at her mother. "He was here just a couple of days ago and he's back already? What the hell is he hanging around for? Can't you find anybody more interesting to screw with? Where's that rich old Mr. Wonderful you had servicing you? What the hell is going on around here? I need something to eat."

She had just pulled herself from the chair when there was a tap on the patio door. It slid open, and Frank leaned in. "Honey," he began, "what do you want—" Then he saw Celia, and she saw him. He froze, then started to back away.

Celia smiled, licking her lips with her mouth still open. She set her high-heeled feet wide apart on the carpet and put both hands on her barely covered hips. "Good morning, New Mr. Wonderful," she said. "Come on in where's it's warm—" she wiggled her hips, "—and cozy." She tipped her head, narrowed her eyes, and said, "Or are you too wussy?"

Pat grabbed the afghan from Priscilla's sleeping legs and threw it over Celia's shoulders. "Get upstairs, Celia!" She pushed at her daughter's tall body. "Get out!"

"Oh, Mama!" Celia said. "You're hurting poor little Celia." She tore the afghan from her shoulders and threw it back at Pat. "Get out? You want me to get out?" She reached for the knob on the front door, turned it, and stepped out onto the porch. "Hey, everybody!" she shouted. "My mother is throwing me out! My mother wants her boyfriend to herself. Anybody interested in a discarded not-quite-virginal woman?"

"Dear God," Pat whispered, and as she reached to pull her daughter back inside, Celia turned. "Don't touch me!" she said. "Don't even think of touching me." She shoved Pat aside and stomped back into the house, back across the living room, and into Pat's studio. "My mother, the renowned, world-famous, who-the-hell-cares stained glass cutter. My mother," she swept from Pat's work table and onto the floor the pieces of glass that Pat had begun assembling for the church window. She took hold of a large sheet of streaked purple glass that was leaning against the wall, and she threw it onto the floor. "That's what I think of your lousy stained glass," she said. She found another sheet, this one a mixture of green and gold and brown, and this one she punched, and it broke in two, the pieces shattering as they hit the tiled floor. "I hate this goddamned glass," she said. "I hate every goddamned inch of your goddamned glass."

Frank was behind her now, and he pinned Celia's arms behind her back.

"Ow-w-w," she wailed. "Who the hell—?" She tried to turn, but Frank was too strong.

"Call an ambulance, Pat," Frank said calmly. "Get her medicine and call an ambulance." Celia was struggling, strong, vicious, but Frank held tight. He spoke to her. "If you don't calm down, Celia, you're going to break your own arm."

She kicked back at him, and the spiked heel of her shoe tore his pants and cut his leg, but he did not let go. "I swear, Celia, you are going to hurt yourself or I am going to hurt you, and we'll both be very sorry." She squirmed. He pulled back as Celia fought to free herself. Pat heard her shoulder pop. Then Celia screamed, and Pat ran for the phone.

"Mama!" came Priscilla's tiny voice from the living room. "Mama!"

"It's okay, sweetheart," Pat was saying as she dialed. "Celia's sick, but it's okay You lie still. Don't move, honey," and then she was talking to the dispatcher, giving her a name, an address, and saying, "Hurry!" And then Pat was in the kitchen trying to fill the water glass, trying to shake pills out of the bottle, trying to make her unsteady hands carry them to the studio.

Celia had crumpled, Frank squatting behind her but not having loosened his grip on her. "Now you're going to take your medicine, Celia, and you're going to sit right here on the floor until we get you some help." His voice was steady and strong. He let go of Celia's arms and put his hands gently on her shoulders. He turned to Pat. "Give it to her," he said.

Celia swallowed the pills, and she let Frank check her shoulder as she sat there crying, and he said, "I think it dislocated but popped back in. I don't think it's broken, but it will be sore for a few days. We'll have it checked."

Pat, also in tears, brought Celia decent clothes and helped her into them in spite of the injured shoulder. "I love you, honey," she kept saying. "I love you. It will be okay. We'll take care of you. I love you, honey." She brushed Celia's hair and washed the tears from her cheeks.

Still crying, Celia looked up and said in a deep monotone, "I love you, too, Mama."

Within a few minutes Celia was walking in her running shoes to the ambulance. She climbed in and sat down, an attendant on each side of her.

"I'll stay with Priscilla," Frank said, sitting on the edge of the couch and holding the hand of the frightened child. "You go on with Celia. I'll be here when you get back."

As she headed toward the garage, Pat stopped. She crossed the living room and looked out the window at her curbed Outback. "Thank goodness she brought it back in one piece." She stared at Frank. "Where was she?" He could only shake his head.

"Will you be okay, sweetie?" Pat leaned to touch Priscilla's forehead. It was cooler.

The little girl nodded. "Can we start *Snow White* over again?" she asked.

The phone rang again. "Do you want me to answer it?" Frank asked, but Pat got there first.

It was Stephanie. She was crying. "Tracy," she said. "Tracy."

Chapter 12

Frank stayed that night. "Even the minister of your church would understand, honey," he said. As the two of them sat there in the dark on the patio, the debris from the boys' debacle hidden on this moonless night, Pat went down the list in her mind.

1. Celia was under control in the hospital, sedated, waiting to be transferred to a psychiatric unit. Dr. Baltry had actually come. He had urged Pat to sign the papers. She had. Six weeks? A year? Maybe forever? No! Don't even think it, Pat told herself. Just until my little girl is better, Pat told herself.

2. For good or ill, Roswell was gone. There was no point in even trying to find him. He would show up again eventually. For good or ill.

3. Rosella? For all intents and purposes, a stranger.

4. Patricia Tazewell, complainant, had been asked to come to the police station in the morning to make a statement. Mr. Thomas Faurault had again asserted that one Celia Tazewell had been disturbing the peace and destroying housing development property and harassing neighbors, and since that Celia Tazewell was co-habited with Patricia Tazewell but was incompetent to respond to the complaint, Mrs. Patricia Tazewell would have to report to the police on her behalf.

5. At least half of the glass for the church window had been destroyed, but that was a small matter in the larger scheme of things.

6. At Frank's suggestion, Pat had called Jerry, but he had not yet responded to her "Please, please, please call right away" message.

7. Her father was dead, and her mother was dead, and Colin was dead, and poor little innocent Tracy Morrison was dead, dead, dead, dead, dead, and Stephanie Morrison and Jack Morrison were dying of grief and Priscilla Morrison could not possibly understand what was going on.

8. Patricia Tazewell didn't even have enough sense to cry.

"Pastor Sandusky will like the design for the window," Pat said aloud.

Frank squeezed her hand. "Of course he will, honey. It's beautiful."

Pat sighed. "It's broken. The glass is all broken."

"We'll replace it. You can use the broken pieces for something else. I'll clean all that up in the morning."

Pat laughed. "After you clean up the yard and my life."

"While," he said. "And you clean up mine. The Fauraults can pay for the yard. You don't need to do that. Neither do I. Just your studio."

"Okay," she pushed with her feet to set the swing in motion again. "Mr. Sandusky stayed for hours that day he came to visit. He's never even met Celia."

"The hospital called him. He went to see her, and then he went to the Morrisons'."

"Is he there now?" she asked.

"I doubt it. It's pretty late."

They heard an owl hoot down in the woods. "Should I go back over there?" Pat asked.

"Jack said he would call if he needed us—you," Frank reminded her.

"You're staying tonight?" she asked.

"I intend to," he said. "As long as you want."

"How about forever?" She managed to smile in the dark.

"That's a possibility," Frank said.

"I asked Stephanie a long time ago how many children she wanted," Pat remembered. "She said Jack wanted at least three more, but she wasn't sure, maybe one more. She didn't want to lose control like Chloe did." Pat felt as if she couldn't breathe. "She said she'd rather not have any more kids at all than have them end up like Chloe's."

Pat took a deep breath and pushed with her feet to keep the swing moving. "I told her none of us have any assurance, that I did the best I could with mine, and look at them."

Frank turned to take her in his arms. "Oh, honey, don't do this to yourself. You and Colin were great with the kids. You just can't live their lives for them. They make their own mistakes." He bent his head and pressed his cheek against her hair.

Pat leaned against Frank. "And we make ours."

"Someone told me a long time ago something I have tried to live by," Frank offered. "He was the campus minister at Penn State when I was there, and I had tried to be friends with my roommate but couldn't. I thought there was something wrong with me or with the way I was approaching this guy, so I talked to the minister, and he gave me the best advice anyone has ever given me. He just looked me in the eye and said, 'Francis, the Good Lord does not require us to be successful. Only faithful.' You have certainly been faithful, sweetheart—both to the Good Lord and to your kids."

Pat slowly pulled away. "I'm tired. Can you stay?"

Frank nodded. "I said I would. You have a big couch."

"The spare bedroom," Pat said. "Top of the stairs, second on the left. Clean towels in the closet. I think I got rid of most of Roswell's remnants, and I put clean sheets on the bed, but I don't remember vacuuming." She stood unsteadily, and he got up to take her elbow.

"Will you be okay?" he asked.

She didn't answer, instead turning and going through the door and through the kitchen and up the stairs. "I'll stay out here a while," Frank said, but Pat did not respond.

She used the toilet and took a short shower, then went to her bedroom. From her dresser drawer she pulled out an old nightgown, a pale green gown with lace at the neckline and around the cuffs. It had been Colin's favorite.

The closet shelf was high, but Pat scooted the desk chair to the door and climbed up to reach the gold-trimmed, dark blue scrapbook. Back down, she sat on the side of her bed and let the book fall open. A picture from Colin and Pat's wedding, Celia's first baby picture, the infant twins sharing a bassinet, school pictures from first grade through junior high—what had happened after that? Why didn't photographers take school pictures in high school? Perhaps the kids didn't change enough from ninth grade until graduation for their parents to want to pay for the photos.

And then there were the pictures from Wales. Oh, Colin, Wales! That Christmas!

Pat moved the chair back over to the small desk, and, rather than go back downstairs to the computer, rather than disturb Frank, she pulled on a drawer and took out several pieces of flowered stationery that were too flowery for her ever to use for letters. She took a pencil from the center drawer and started writing.

> Rosella and Roswell hadn't been born when Colin and I took Celia and went to Wales for Christmas. I can see Colin's face, a smile as big as a Seneca cave when we got off the train in Cardiff and his whole family—well, most of them—were there to meet us. There must have been forty of them, and Colin handed Celia to me—she was about two and we had been traveling for days, so she was asleep and it was the middle of the night anyway—and Colin began hugging everyone, and everyone was hugging him and me with Celia in my arms, and I have never felt so welcome anywhere in my whole life, not even in my new church here in Tremont City, which is very friendly.
>
> Christmas in Cardiff lasted forever That's what made me fat until I got back home and started going

to the spa and working out to Richard Simmons videotapes at home. We ate pasties and roast lamb and tons of "tatties" and fried apples and, well, it never ended, the food and the fun and the Welsh ale and all. I kept telling my handsome, black-haired, lustful Colin that when we started home, they would be charging him extra luggage because of all the weight I was gaining, but he just laughed and said, "A Welshman likes women, not scarecrows," in that wonderful Welsh accent which I never got tired of and always found highly attractive, and he would pinch me under the table or even in front of his cousins, or he would grab my hips and swing me around the room, and everyone just loved Celia.

Christmas in Wales is not lots of presents like here in this country, but it lasts forever, like well into January and features families and friendships and food, and they go to church a lot.

I know why Colin came to love West Virginia. It and Wales look a lot alike with the hills and all the coal mines, which have mostly shut down now, but we have more trees. Wales and all of the British Isles have had most of the trees cut down and they are just now growing back.

Sitting there at the desk thinking about Colin and Christmas and the warmth of his family home and the people, Pat dozed. Then the telephone rang, and she picked up the extension there on her desk. It was Jerry, but he was too late. Pat said, "I can't talk now. I'll call you tomorrow or the next day after the funeral."

"What funeral?" he asked.

"Stephanie's baby," she said. "Their two-month-old baby. He died of meningitis. I can't talk about it. Please," she said.

"Oh, Mrs. Patsy," Jerry said, "I am highly sorrowful. I will send flowers to Stephanie and Jack Morrison. I will call you another day."

"Good night," Pat said and hung up. She needed to go to bed, she thought. She needed not to think about that cold, still baby. She needed not to think about Stephanie and Jack holding each other in the dark, the very, very dark house. She needed not to think about poor little Priscilla not understanding a single thing that was going on except that her little brother who was too sick had gone to heaven where he wouldn't be sick anymore. "Oh, God," Pat breathed.

She needed to go to bed, but she looked down at what she had written, and she picked up the pencil again.

The people in Wales look a lot like West Virginians except there are not as many fat women. The men are thin and generally gray-looking from the mines and all, and there is a higher percentage of deaths in Welsh mines because they aren't very careful.

That's what I think Christmas should be—families and friends and fun. And, of course, Jesus, which all of us sometimes tend to forget including the Welsh people although they cross themselves a lot. I am glad Colin decided to become a Baptist even though that was one thing his family did not like at all, but Colin and I just went to their Catholic church with them and didn't say anything about it, but they knew, especially because I didn't know all the things they were saying in church and I didn't know when to kneel and all. Colin still took communion. Maybe he still believed it was really Jesus' blood and body. I don't.

Christmas in Wales that time was very, very special, so much better than here where you listen to the same old "Rudolph the Red-nosed Reindeer" every day after Halloween and then you watch children's choirs on TV from after Thanksgiving or the soap operas with their everlasting Susan Luccis and their thousand-dollar gowns which they change every day

and which leave nothing to the imagination in terms
of their bony or buxom bosoms and their make-up-
encrusted faces and their supposedly crystal punch
bowls with what is supposed to be champagne but is
at best stale ginger ale which spills down the front of
the thousand-dollar gowns to give the aging and
slightly paunchy but still handsome leading men
excuses to pull out their supposedly linen
handkerchiefs to apologize profusely and wipe away
the stains and the ever-present tears of the recently
bereaved but heroically brave leading women who are
either getting too old to be leading women or who are
so young that they ought to be in school instead of on
a television set. And they all act like there's intrigue
hanging from the chandeliers along with the fake
mistletoe, but the only question in my mind is why
these people get paid more than miners or school
teachers or policemen. That's the crime, not all that
stuff the writers have to come up with and burn
themselves out on and even commit suicide. But that's
beside the point of this piece I am writing.

Christmas. Welsh people understand Christmas
better than we do, and they do better birthdays, too.
Colin helped me with that. We kind of used to go
overboard on birthdays even though we weren't as
bad as lots of people I know who give each other and
their kids (maybe that's why we have so many
delinquents around these days like the Faurault boys)
cars and diamonds and trips to Paris and all like that.

Why, I remember one of my birthdays, the very
first one after Colin and I were married, I think, and I
don't even have a picture in the album of it because
we didn't own a camera until Celia was born, and
Mama couldn't come from Durbin because she was
still running the B&B, and Colin and I had just come

from the every-year Thanksgiving football game which the miners played on every holiday except in the summer when they played baseball instead and did very well with leagues and contests and tournaments and all. That was a lot of fun, those baseball games with all the families on the sidelines and the kids running around behind the bleachers that the miners had built, the kids playing tag or catch or whatever, and Colin's team was very good and even had uniforms and caps with their name on them— Hot Diggers!

But my birthday was on that Thanksgiving, too, and Colin and I came home and were sitting together on that miserable, rock-hard excuse for a couch, snuggling and drinking stale Coke instead of champagne like on the soap operas, and we had no money for presents, but I had made pasties and butter cakes like he used to have in Wales and he had given me a silver necklace that had a little silver cross on it that he said his mother had given it to him to give to me on a special occasion, and I still wear it all the time, and I said, "This is the most beautiful present I have ever received, and I wish I had something equally meaningful to give to you," and he said, "You are my present, Patsy. You are all the present I will ever want or need," and he was right. I was his best present, and he was mine, thank you, God. After that we went for a long walk and found a stray apple tree with apples still on it and on the ground that were good enough for applesauce, which I made when we got back to the trailer and which was the most delicious applesauce I have ever, ever eaten. Oh, my beloved Colin, I want to go back! I want to be who I was and we were. I feel as lonely and as useless as a scarecrow in a cucumber patch. I want to be—

Pat stopped writing. Frank was flushing the toilet in the downstairs bathroom. She looked down at the paper. For heaven's sake! She told herself. She could never, ever, show this to anyone, not even Fonzie. Stupid! Stupid! Stupid! Why did she ever get started on all this remembering nonsense? Why had she agreed to—.

She straightened up. She was useless? Not unless there was no one in the whole wide world who needed her help or her company or her applesauce or her brownies. Lonely is what is truly stupid. That doesn't happen if you're useful.

She tore up the last two sheets of paper, saving most of the Wales story. That part was okay, she told herself. "Come on, Patricia Tazewell," she said aloud. "Get to bed."

She did, and she slept, and when she woke the next morning, the sun was shining, and she could hear someone in the backyard. Not those boys again!

Grabbing a sweatshirt—Baltimore Ravens, not Mickey Mouse— she pulled it on and went out onto the balcony. Then she smiled. It was Frank. He had found coveralls somewhere and was working on the mountain of trash. "Good morning," Pat called. "I thought we were going to hire someone and let the insurance company pay the bill."

He waved up to her. "I couldn't stand it. If you're going to use the patio in the next six months, which is probably how long it will take the insurance company to get around to you, you won't want to keep being reminded of this mess. You can still make them pay for new grass and flowers."

"I'll be right down to help."

"Right down," he said, "fine. Help, no. Go check on Stephanie."

She nodded and went back inside, pulled off the sweatshirt and her nightgown. She folded the gown and dressed. Scooting the desk chair back over to the closet; she climbed up and laid the gown on top of the scrapbook she had put back sometime last night. Frank would want to see the pictures sometime, but not now. "Got to move on, Colin, my love," she whispered. "Time *fugits. De gustibus* or whatever they say. You know what I mean."

She hopped back down and went to the bathroom to brush her teeth, pull her hair back into a bun, and put on make-up. Looking into the mirror, she said, "Not too bad for an old woman. Chin up, shoulders back, stiff upper lip." Faking a Greta Garbo tone, she said, "Attitude, my dear, is everything."

On the kitchen table she found a clipping from a newspaper or magazine. It read, "All of the tomorrows of all of our lives must first go through the hands of God." She went to the patio door and opened it. "You left this for me?"

Frank turned and smiled at her. "Billy Graham thought you could use a little reminder."

"He was right," she said. "So are you. Coffee in three minutes. I'll start it and go over to the Morrisons' and be right back."

Ralph Sandusky was with Stephanie and Jack. Priscilla's fever was completely gone. Pat took the little girl's hand and led her back across the road. "What would you like to do today, honey?" Pat asked.

"I want to go far away," Priscilla said firmly. "I don't like people sad."

Pat looked down at her. "You're right. Let's ask Frank where we can go."

"Not the zoo," Priscilla said. "I'm tired of elephants." She swung Pat's hand in hers. Then she stopped in the middle of the road. "Is Celia home?"

Pat squatted there in the street. "No, sweetheart. She's sick. She's in the hospital."

"Is she going to be dead, too?" Priscilla backed away but still held Pat's hand.

"Definitely not," Pat said. "She is getting well. The doctor says she will be all well soon and won't be mean anymore."

"Good." Priscilla started walking again, and then she let go of Pat's hand and ran around the house to where Frank was. As soon as he saw her, he threw toward the woods the armload of trash he was carrying. "Hey!" he said. "How's our girl?"

"Fine," she said, and she ran to hug his knees. "You are going to take me somewhere."

He looked up at Pat and raised his eyebrows, "That's great. Where is somewhere?"

"We haven't decided," Priscilla said. She turned to Pat. "Not a movie. I'm tired of movies, especially *Snow White*."

"A playground?" Pat asked.

"Swings are boring," Priscilla said.

"A park?" Pat asked.

Priscilla shook her head. "No swings. I'm hungry."

"That's the best idea I've heard all morning," Frank said. "Unplug the coffee, Mrs. Tazewell," he said, and he started to unbutton his coveralls.

"Where did you get that charming outfit?" Pat asked.

"The trunk of my car. Never know when I'm going to have the opportunity to change some gorgeous woman's tire," he grinned. "Let's go eat."

They went to the diner out on the highway, and Priscilla ate as if she had just discovered food. "Where are we going next?" she asked.

"I have a suggestion," Pat said. She leaned toward the little girl. "You are such a good glass artist, how would you like to see how glass is made? We have to go the other direction, so let's go back to my house. We'll tell your mom and dad where we're going, and I need to call Celia, and then we'll head for the hills."

"Glass is in the hills?" Priscilla asked.

"Sort of," Pat said as she smoothed Priscilla's beautiful hair. "Let's go, kiddo!"

Chapter 13

But before they could leave again, Dolly was at Pat's front door. "Are you okay?" she asked. "I just came from Stephanie's house. She asked me to check on Priscilla and you."

"I was going to stop over there. We're about to leave for the day, get Priscilla away for a while. Her fever is gone, and she's raring to go."

"Good idea." She looked closely at Pat. "You look tired. Have you heard from Celia?"

"She's in better hands than mine," Pat smiled weakly. "I talked to a nurse just now. She'll be okay. She'll get better."

"Can you step outside for a minute?" Dolly asked.

"Would you like to come in?"

"No—outside," Dolly insisted. "I need to—Walker is on his way to see Celia."

"How did he find out where she is? I wasn't going to tell anyone."

"He got to the hospital just after the ambulance left, and someone in the ER told him where they were headed."

"They shouldn't have."

Dolly took Pat's hand and led her onto the porch, then pulled the door closed behind her. "He would have told you, but what with Tracy and all—. He left first thing this morning."

"Why? I don't understand. Who is he anyway?" Pat asked.

"That's what I wanted to tell you. Let's sit down." She lowered herself onto the step and Pat followed her. "Walker came to me well over a year ago," Dolly said. "He had gotten hooked on heroin and needed help."

"He's a dope addict?" Pat stared at Dolly. "I thought he was—"

"Recovering," Dolly said. "When I met him, he had already been through rehab, and he wanted help staying off the stuff. He was never as bad as some addicts get."

"Has he really stopped?" Pat asked.

"Completely. He has become one of my counselors. I pay him a little, and he has some personal income. He's an excellent counselor. He's been taking some courses at the college in Beckley, and I'm going to be recommending him for counseling jobs as they come up."

"What has all this to do with Celia? They've been spending time together?"

"More than that, Pat," Dolly smiled. "They say they're in love."

"You're kidding! Celia hasn't—"

"She was afraid you wouldn't approve."

Pat snickered. "I've even been putting four-leaf clovers in her shoes in hopes that she would meet the right man. Walker?"

"Could be," Dolly said. She straightened her denim skirt under her and patted Pat's knee. "Celia is a very capable person when she's under control."

"I know," Pat said. "And I've seen how well Walker handles Celia. And," she added, "he's certainly handsome. I just wish I knew—"

"Don't we all?" Dolly said. "But you've got to let go, Pat. Celia needs to take care of her own life. She needs to take her medicine, and she needs to get a job and keep it, and she needs to treat you with respect and gratitude."

Pat stared at her again. "How do you know all this?"

"Stephanie asked me to talk to Celia when I had a chance, and she and Walker have been giving me lots of chances."

The door opened behind them. "I'm becoming rather impatient," Priscilla announced.

Dolly turned. "I'll bet you got those words from Mrs. Tazewell's friend."

"Some of them," Priscilla admitted.

Pat stood, reaching to help Dolly up from the low step. Then she hugged Dolly, and Dolly hugged back. "It will be okay, Pat. You'll see. Go try to have a good time. I'll keep an eye on our neighbors."

"My friend has cleaned up most of the backyard," Pat said. "I sure hope those boys don't get any more bright ideas."

"I meant the Morrisons," Dolly said as she turned to leave, "but you're right. If that gang attacked you, they could just as well pick on the rest of us. They call it 'tagging' these days—vandalism with or without spray cans of paint. I'll keep my eyes open."

"Come on, please," Priscilla said again. Frank was standing behind her and waved to Dolly, who waved back and went on her way.

Priscilla was running down the sidewalk to Frank's car, and Pat went back inside just long enough to get her pocketbook. Then here came Dolly back, carrying a car seat and three books for Priscilla.

Finally they were on their way, Frank whistling and Priscilla singing, "Hi-ho, hi-ho." When they ran out of song, Frank turned and laid his hand on Pat's leg. "Which way, boss?"

"She's not your boss," Priscilla said from the back seat.

"That's what you think," Frank laughed. "Tell us where we're going," he told Pat.

"To Huntington," she said. "Two or three glass plants there. First Blenko. I need to see whether they can supply a piece I need for the center of the Marlinton window."

"The restoration project," Frank remembered.

Pat nodded. "It took me hours and hours to go through records, dirty, dusty, very valuable records, like they were written by hand, and most of them were in bound volumes of one kind or another." She turned back to Priscilla. "Do you know what people used before we had Scotch tape?"

Priscilla frowned without looking up from her first book. "Band-aids?" she asked.

Pat laughed. "Almost." She turned back to Frank. "Do you know?"

"I remember my mother and dad using brown paper tape, and I am familiar with paper clips."

"Some of the records I looked at had been fastened with straight pins that are now all rusty. Some pages had actually been sewn together by hand. Like invoices stitched to minutes, that kind of thing."

"I'll bet the person taking the minutes was a woman," Frank suggested.

"Wrong," Pat said. "Men ran everything. Including being secretaries of organizations and clerks of cities and counties. Not many women's names on any of the documents I looked at."

"But," Frank said, "I'll bet they were not very far behind the scenes. They probably did the sewing part. What were you looking for?"

"Where they were getting their glass back then and who designed and installed the windows in Marlinton and Nicholas County. And sure enough, almost all of the glass came from West Virginia, mostly Wissmach over on the Ohio River, but Wissmach can't replace the glass jewel that was at the very middle of the Marlinton window."

"Do you have to be on-site to do the work?"

"For Marlinton, yes, after I pattern and cut some of the broken pieces. That I can do at home. I haven't been doing much of anything these last few months, though. The window is pretty well finished, but the church has put me on hold because the committee can't reach an agreement as to how to give credit to those who have paid for the restoration." She laid her hand on top of Frank's and looked out at the Catholic church they were just passing. The windows, very modern in design, sparkled in the sunlight.

"Don't they think the credit should go to God?" Frank suggested. "He doesn't need an inscription or a plaque, and neither should his children."

"I'm a children," Priscilla said, her voice sounding soft and distant.

"You certainly are, honey," Pat said. She turned back to Frank. "I've also been asked to work on the restoration of a church in New Martinsville, but that's also on the Ohio near Paden City where the Wissmach plant is, and I'd have to be over there a lot, and I just can't be away from Celia that long."

"This might be just the time to do it," Frank suggested.

She tipped her head. "Maybe. They don't need an answer this minute, so I guess I'll just see what happens. They're willing to pay well, and I could make good use of the money." She paused, wanting to reassure him. "Actually, though, I'm not hurting for income. I've been asked to do some windows for a bank in Bluefield, interior windows, which don't thrill me— artificial lighting behind them and all like that. But I've also had a call from some people building a great big house down at the lake beyond Dr. Baltry's and Jamie's places, and I may take that job if I can just bring myself to drive back and forth along that road. What if Jamie came back and saw me?"

Frank looked at her. "What if he did?"

"I don't know," Pat said. "I just don't know what I'd do. Probably spit in his face."

A small voice came from behind them. "Mommy says spitting is not nice. I don't want you to talk about spitting."

"How about glass?" Pat asked. "Should I tell Mr. Frank about how glass is made?"

Priscilla agreed.

"Here comes a lecture," Pat said.

"Go for it," Frank agreed as he turned toward I-64 and Huntington.

She talked about the discovery of glass by ancient sailors. She talked about the Egyptians making jewelry with glass to imitate precious stones. She talked about the years of labor that went into the building of the cathedrals in Europe and how most of the stained glass was destroyed by the Puritans during the Reformation. She talked about American glass, Tiffany and La Farge. "And did you know," she asked, "there were once about five hundred glass plants in West Virginia?"

Frank shook his head. "Now?"

"About a dozen," Pat said. "Only three or four big ones."

"Sad," Frank said.

She kept talking, and he kept listening, and Priscilla kept reading her books, possibly also listening, until there they were, in the parking lot at the Blenko factory. The pale building gleamed in the bright daylight, the trees and shrubs green around it. Priscilla hopped out of the car as soon as she was unbuckled, and Pat took her hand. "You need to stay very close," Pat said. "There are lots of things that can break if you touch them."

"I know," Priscilla said, flipping her braids and waiting for Frank to take her other hand. "They're glass like at your house."

"Some of it is like my glass," Pat agreed, "but at this factory they make mostly fancy vases and bowls and lumps of glass like in Jerry's front door."

"I noticed that," Frank said.

"Dalle de verre," Pat said. "Tiffany wanted something unusual, something heavy and impressive. That's dalle de verre You have to have a very heavy frame for it."

"Like in the walls of big buildings," Frank said. "I've never seen it in the door of a private home before."

"Tiffany didn't want cathedral glass—the flat kind. She had to be different. And," Pat laughed, "she sure was."

"Tiffany has pretty clothes," Priscilla said. She pulled free from Pat in order to point at a medallion hanging in the front window of the showroom. "That looks like a dog eating a squirrel," she said.

Pat laughed. "I don't think that's what the artist had in mind, but you can see whatever you want to see."

"That one," Priscilla pointed at another medallion, "looks like Tracy going to heaven."

Pat looked at the glass, then at Frank. He lifted his eyebrows and said, "It's a very nice idea, young lady. The person who made it would like that."

"I have to go to the bathroom," Priscilla said.

That taken care of, the three of them, with Frank carrying Priscilla so that she could see, walked across the closed-in bridge that led from the showroom to the factory.

They stood at the wooden railing and wondered at the open mouths of the furnaces. They saw the glass drawn on pipes from the furnaces, watched the helpers carry the hot glass to the blowers, watched the blowers shape objects from the molten glass and then cool them in tubs of water. They watched the helpers carry the hot glass to the cooling ovens. It was too noisy to talk. Finally they walked back across the bridge, stopping to wonder at the mountain of scrap glass lying in the yard between two factory buildings. "What will become of that?" Frank asked. "Surely they don't throw it out."

"Do they have a recycle basket?" Priscilla asked.

"It's recycled, all right," Pat smiled up at the little girl. "They'll put it back into the furnaces with the new glass, and it gets mixed in, and that way it doesn't ever get thrown away." She turned to Frank. "That's why it's hard to recreate a glass that has had scraps thrown in. Every batch is different, and that's the way they made most of the glass in olden times, so it's very hard to replace. Now most of it is mixed by formula. Computerized."

"My daddy says everybody should recycle," Priscilla declared. "Is that what happens when Mommy takes our old bottles to the center?" she asked.

"Almost," Pat said. "You know, Priscilla, you are almost too smart for your own good."

"What's that?" she asked.

"Help!" Pat said to Frank. "It's your turn."

"Tell you what, little lady. I'll let you down if you promise not to touch, and you can pick out something to take home to your mother and dad."

"I don't have any money," Priscilla said as she swung down from Frank's arms.

"I do," he offered. "I think I have enough for you to get your mom a present and enough for us to get something to eat and—"

"McDonald's?"

"How about it, Mrs. Tazewell?" Frank asked. "McDonald's okay?"

"Your mom doesn't like McDonald's very well, honey," Pat said.

"Mommy isn't here," Priscilla reminded her.

"True," Pat smiled. "Okay, McDonald's it will be. What shall we take to your mom and dad?"

"Hamburgers," Priscilla suggested. Even the showroom clerk laughed. The young woman came from behind the counter and took Priscilla's hand. "I'll bet your mama would like a pretty bowl for her table," she said.

"Do you have a little girl?" Priscilla asked.

The girl nodded. "Tiffany," she said, "and she is just a little older than you are."

Priscilla turned to Pat with wide eyes. "Tiffany?"

"A different Tiffany, honey," Pat said. She followed as the clerk and Priscilla led the way.

"Mama doesn't want a bowl," Priscilla stated.

"How about a vase?" Frank asked.

"Mama doesn't want a vase. She has too many already." Priscilla said.

Pat looked at Frank and shrugged. "What do you think she would like?" she asked.

"Tracy going to heaven," Priscilla said.

The clerk turned to look at Pat, who just shook her head and smiled. "That would be a beautiful present," Frank said, and he went to take the medallion from the window.

"That's all?" Frank asked. "Pat? How about a dog eating a dead squirrel?"

"Not today," she said. "No squirrels or monkeys. We have another place to stop, and then it will be time to head back."

"McDonald's," Priscilla said. She let go of the clerk's hand and took Pat's. "You promised."

"Yeah, yeah, yeah," Pat said as she knelt to hug Priscilla. "McDonald's and then one other place, okay?"

"After McDonald's."

They found a tiny factory near Huntington, just one blower, one helper, one clerk. The three visitors watched again, this time very close, as the glass blower, using tiny blobs of glass and a narrow blow pipe, turned out perfume vial after perfume vial in varicolored glass. "How does he do that?" Priscilla asked. "Does he have the colors in his mouth?"

"The colors are in the glass when it comes from the furnace," Pat smiled.

"It's a little furnace for so many colors," the little girl said. "All those colors in those things in the store?"

"Not all at once," said the clerk who had accompanied them. "Would you like to see some unusual products?" she asked Frank.

They saw the finished perfume vials with their tiny stoppers. They saw multi-colored birds—cardinals, blue jays, owls, orioles— all shaped by the on-site blower plus another craftsman who wasn't working today. Then Priscilla spied a gourd-shaped object with a hole in it. "What's that?" she asked.

"A hummingbird feeder," the clerk said.

"Can I have one?" Priscilla looked up at Frank.

"Wouldn't you rather have something for your very own room?" he asked.

"I want a feeder for my very own hummingbirds," she said, her lips tight.

"You got it," Frank smiled. "Which color?"

Priscilla picked out a pink and green and white one. "My hummers will like this. Thank you very much," she said. "Can you make one like this?" she asked Pat.

"Nope. I don't have a blower," Pat said.

"You should get one," Priscilla suggested. "These are cool."

Pat turned to Frank. "We'd better go. Stephanie will start to worry."

"You can call her from the car," Frank offered.

Pat tried, but the line was busy. "Probably getting ready for tomorrow," Pat said. The funeral. The good-byes for Tracy. How could they all get through it? And what about Priscilla?

Pat looked into the back seat. They had left the glass shop just ten minutes earlier, but the little girl was sound asleep. "Thank God," Pat said quietly, "her fever disappeared. Wouldn't it be terrible—" She couldn't even say it.

"She's fine," Frank said. "Her fever wasn't the same thing, honey. Why don't you lean the seat back and take a nap yourself? You've had a tough few days, and they aren't over yet."

She leaned back and closed her eyes. Think good thoughts, she told herself. Think beautiful windows and lovely birdfeeders and—. She came awake suddenly. "Oh, Frank," she said, "I forgot the jewel for the Marlinton window."

"Want to go back?"

"Not today. Not with Priscilla. I'll call. They know me in the office, at least by name." She leaned back again, clearing her mind, thinking this time about all the people she loved, all of the people who had problems of their own, all of the people she was praying for—Celia and Roswell and Rosella and Stephanie and Jack and Dolly and Walker and those clients of Dolly's and Priscilla and Tracy, bless his little soul, and Jerry and oh, yes, Frank. He was surely one of those sneaky little tricks of God that Ralph Sandusky talked about. Porter Jamison? Forget him! She leaned her head against Frank's strong shoulder and fell asleep.

Chapter 14

The funeral was over. Tracy's tiny body had been buried in a white casket covered with white roses. The church had been festooned with more roses plus baby's breath, white satin ribbons and ceramic lambs. Pastor Sandusky had kept the service mercifully short. After all, what could one say? It wasn't as if Tracy had been born with disabilities, and it wasn't as if he had been sick for a long time. No one is ever ready for death. But in the case of Tracy John Morrison, there hadn't even been two months or even two weeks or even two full days to prepare anyone. Even Pastor Sandusky was left with virtually no words.

The hardest part of the service and the most beautiful was the singing of the children's choir, "Jesus Loves Me," "Sunshine and Rain, Happiness and Pain," and "Jesus Loves the Little Children." Afterwards, as Jack stood at the door holding Priscilla in his arms and thanking those who had come to share the Morrisons' grief, someone said to Priscilla, "We're sorry you lost your little brother." She frowned at the speaker and said, "He's not lost. He's with Jesus."

"You're right," the woman in the big brown hat said. "Of course you're right, but we hope you won't be lonely."

Priscilla shook her head and said, "I can talk to him every day, and I am going to ask God to make sure he's better."

What, indeed, could anyone say?

Frank had stayed and gone to the funeral, mainly to support Pat, but she hadn't wanted to make him attend the burial. Instead they had stopped at the Morrisons' to start the coffee urn and then to make sure Stephanie did not need help with her family members and the friends who would stop by. Jack's family had not shown up.

Frank commented on how beautiful their front door was with the sunlight coming through, how the birches and sycamores that Pat had designed into the window blended perfectly with the woods across the road and behind the house. "You are so, so good," he told Pat, "and I don't mean just with glass."

There were three messages on the machine when they got to the Tazewell house. One was from Celia's hospital, asking Pat to call immediately. The second was from Jessie Miller, who had also asked Pat to call back soon. The third was from Nancy O'Connell, and she was not happy. "Patricia Tazewell," her message said, "I know you and Frank are there, and I know what you are trying to do. I am told that ours is not the first marriage you have tried to destroy. This is a warning. If you do not stop seducing my husband, you are going to be very, very sorry. And yes, this is a threat. Call the police. Call the army. Call the President of the United States and every damned judge on the Supreme Court. This is a threat. If you do not stop, I will see that you are stopped." She had hung up.

Pat stared at the telephone, trying to imagine Nancy's face, trying to imagine where she was, who might be with her, what stories she had been telling to whomever she could get to listen. Then Pat turned to Frank, who was standing frozen behind her. "I am so sorry," he whispered at last. He reached for her, but she backed away.

There was a long silence, the two of them looking hard at each other, and then Pat said, "I think you'd better go home."

He hesitated, then nodded. "I will, sweetheart, but not until we talk. Call the hospital first."

She shook her head, her eyes closing. "Not yet," Pat said. She was so tired. Dear God, she did not need this Nancy stuff. She just wanted to hear that Celia was much better, even after so little time. She wanted to forget about Jessie Miller's call. She wanted to forget about Tracy dying. She wanted to be alone. But Frank looked so sad, and she loved him.

He followed her into the kitchen, bright yellow with late afternoon sun. It was almost as if God himself were telling her to smile, to be happy,—about what? She sat down hard in one of the chairs. Frank sat in another. "Do you want something to eat?" she asked.

He shook his head. "I'll be gone in a minute," he said, "but first I have to tell you something."

She waited, not curious, not caring, just waiting.

"I've filed for a divorce," he said. "My lawyer is working on the papers," he smiled slightly, "even as we speak. Nancy and I were through with each other a long time ago, and it's way past time to admit it."

"That's not what she thinks," Pat said.

Frank shrugged. "That's what she wants you to think. That's how she is. One minute she's telling me to get out and never come back, and the next minute she's threatening to destroy me if I so much as look cross-eyed at the paper boy. Nancy has always wanted to have her cake and eat it, too, and at this particular moment, I guess I'm the cake."

"That's too bad," Pat said, not knowing what else to say, not wanting to say anything. This could not possibly be Patsy Yokum sitting here, Patsy Yokum Tazewell, Pat whoever-whatever-however. Too much! She felt her temperature rising "You'd better go home," she said again. "I'm getting really mad."

"At Nancy or at me?" he asked.

"Both of you. Mainly you," she admitted.

"Because?" he asked.

She was, indeed, angry. "You know, Celia called you a wuss the other day, and she's right. Why the hell do you let Nancy run your life?" She grunted and raised her shoulders. "And why the hell didn't I slap the shit out of her years ago?" She laughed. "I guess I'm as mad at myself as I am at you. I should have—we should have—oh, shoot. Go home."

She had heard those words herself a long time before—some forty years before. They had all still been in high school, seniors, and Pat and Fonzie were sitting next to each other in a booth at The Hop. Two classmates, Jim and Nicky, were there, too. To the accompaniment of the juke box, Nicky had just told a joke about blonds, and all four of them were laughing hard. And then they heard Nancy's voice, and there she was in her pink Garland sweater, her Spaulding saddle shoes, her Bonnie Doone socks—the uniform of the rich girls. There she was, her face red with rage, her blond hair rigid in its spray-fixed pageboy cut, her eyes cutting right through

Patsy's. While two of her girlfriends smirked behind her, Nancy's voice came down on the booth like a coal mine roof-fall. "I'll bet," she said to Patsy, "you like Jew jokes, too."

The laughing stopped. "Aw, Nancy," Nicky had said.

"Sorry," Fonzie offered. "We didn't—"

"Well?" Nancy had demanded of Patsy.

"Everybody tells blond jokes," Pat said, far more calmly than she felt. "We weren't talking about you."

"Everybody does not," Nancy argued. "Not when I'm around." She crossed her arms over her chest, and she licked her glossy lips. "I expect an apology. Right here, right now. From you," she had said, pointing a manicured finger at Pat.

Pat could taste disgust. Sure, the joke had been a bad idea. "We said we were sorry," she said," and it's not like Jew or Pollack jokes, and you have no reason to take it personally. We have already apologized, and I've certainly heard you telling jokes about hippies and hillbillies. I haven't seen anyone taking those personally. We weren't laughing at you, Nancy." She stood. "No one would dare laugh at you, at least not in public."

Nancy had reached out and slapped Pat's face, and before stunned Pat could react, the whole place had erupted, with the manager of The Hop telling all seven of them to go home. They did. At least Pat did, but not before she told Nancy that if she ever touched Pat again, the army would be called in.

By the time it was all over and all the exaggerated stories had been told, with the two groups separating permanently, Nancy had taken her revenge. She had reeled Fonzie in with sex and money as her lures. She even claimed to be pregnant, and Fonzie married her right after graduation. There had never been a baby, of course. And the one time Pat tried to mend her friendship with Fonzie by inviting him to join her on a hike up the river, Nancy was waiting at the end of the trail. She ordered Fonzie into her car, and he had succumbed, and she said to Pat, "It's not safe to hike all alone, Patsy Yokum. You'd better get home to your hillbilly mama." Fonzie had started to get back out of the car, but Nancy zoomed off, leaving Pat eating dust.

Frank nodded now, his thick hair still smooth, shiny, his tired, lined face still so handsome, his hands reaching out so warm, so inviting. But she did not move. He drew his hands back and straightened up in the chair. "Pat," he said, "you know I love you."

She nodded.

"You know I love being with you."

She nodded again.

"And I would like nothing better, I want nothing more in this whole world than to stay right here. You know that."

She shrugged. "You're married," she said.

"For now," he said.

She shrugged again.

Frank stood. "I'm going, sweetheart, but I'll be back as soon as I possibly can. Is there anything I can do before I go?"

She shook her head.

"I'll wait until you call the hospital."

She shook her head again. "It's my problem."

"Get some rest," Frank said as he stood. "I'm going to stop at Dolly's to ask her to keep an eye on you." Then he came around the table, leaned to kiss her on the mouth, and rose again. "I love you, Pat," he said once more.

She nodded and watched him go into the bathroom. She heard him flush the toilet. She heard him wash his hands, and she watched him go out the front door.

Then she laid her head down on her arms on the table and tried to cry, but she couldn't. She could feel her toes inside her good shoes. She could feel her long hair tickling her bare arms. She could feel her tongue in her mouth and her breath going in and out of her lungs, but she couldn't cry.

And then someone was at the front door. Frank had come back? She hoped not. Jerry? No. Roswell was back? Good Lord, no! She got up as the chimes replayed the first notes of "Going Home," and she went to the door.

It was Dolly. Pat stepped aside and let her in. "I have something to tell you," Dolly said. She was still wearing the dark green suit she had worn to the funeral, but she kicked off her mud-flecked high heels. "I stayed for the burial, the interment," she said. "Who's that Frank? He said—."

"Forget it." Pat led the way to the kitchen, her happy room, her not-always-happy room. "Do you want some coffee? I do."

Dolly grunted. "I'd prefer something worth drinking."

Pat looked at her in surprise but opened the cupboard and reached up to the top shelf. "Rum? Scotch? There's probably some wine in the refrigerator."

"Something strong," Dolly said. "Scotch. And pour yourself one."

Pat set the bottle on the table and stopped moving. Celia. That was why Dolly had come. "I have to call the hospital," she said. Now what, Lord? Now what?

Dolly nodded. "Did they call you?"

"While we were gone. I haven't—."

"They left me a message, too. I called," Dolly said. She reached into the cupboard. "Glasses," she said as she brought two. "I'll pour," and she did, hefty portions. "I think we're supposed to just sip this for best effect." She put the bottle on the counter and picked up her glass. "Here's to Celia and Walker," she said.

"Now what?" Pat heard the annoyance in her own voice.

"The hospital said Celia is gone. She signed herself out."

"Oh, God," Pat sighed. "She wasn't supposed to be able to do that."

"I know, but some young twit didn't know or didn't want to know and has subsequently lost her job."

"Where is Celia?" Pat demanded.

"Nobody knows, but there was a man with her. They left in his car, the girl said."

"Walker?"

"Of course. I told the hospital I'd come over and tell you."

"Why did the hospital call you?" Pat asked.

"Walker told them to if they couldn't find you."

Pat sat down hard. "Celia didn't have any medicine with her."

Dolly sat next to her and picked up Pat's glass. "Drink," she said. "Slowly."

Pat did. Then she said again, "Celia didn't have any medicine with her. It's all upstairs."

Dolly frowned and shook her head. "You told me you put it in her pocketbook."

Pat closed her eyes and reopened them, remembering the dramatic scene with the ambulance. "That's right. I did," she said. "Wouldn't they have taken it from her?"

"They should have, but who knows? Maybe some other little twit fouled up." Dolly took Pat's hand and raised it and the glass to Pat's mouth. "Drink," she said again.

"Then all we can do is wait?" Pat asked after she swallowed, shivering.

"If Walker is with her, she'll be okay He really does love her."

"I sincerely hope so." Pat frowned slowly. "You know, I don't even know his last name, do I?" She watched Dolly take another sip of her drink. "I don't know anything about him—or much about you."

"Lottreau," Dolly said. "He's originally from Montreal, and his last name is Lottreau, and he was the manager of Waldenbooks in Charleston before he moved here, and he is writing a book about a revenuer who chased moonshiners in Kentucky and New Jersey and then became governor of West Virginia." Dolly stopped to look at what was left in her glass, then continued. "Walker is independently wealthy. His mother and father were English and were Earl or Lord and Lady or something or other, but Walker refused the title so it went to his brother and he came to Canada."

"Huh! That story smells as bad as rotten fish," Pat said. "I don't believe a word of it." She lifted her glass but decided she wanted no more alcohol. She set it down again.

"It's true," Dolly nodded. "I checked it out because I didn't want a liar for a client—but Walker is for real. It's true." The Scotch was beginning to blur her words. "He'll take care of Celia. You'll see. I've got to go. I've got three wild ones at my house and no Walker. I sure could use him about now. And I've got to check in at the clinic.

Oh, woe!" she said as she drained her glass and rose.

"Could I help?" Pat asked, not really meaning it.

"I'll manage," Dolly smiled tightly. "Call me if you hear anything." She retrieved her shoes and, carrying them, left.

Pat picked up her glass, stood, and went to the sink to pour the Scotch back into the bottle. "It's got to be sterile," she said aloud. Then she put the bottle back into the cupboard and said, still aloud, "So what shall we do while we wait, Patricia Tazewell? One hairy problem after another." She turned full-circle, continuing to talk to herself. "Would you like to work in the yard? No? Would you like to work on the church window? No? How about housecleaning? No? Food? Not on your life. Go for a walk? Maybe. Call Frank? Absolutely not. Jerry? Not today." She stood for a moment looking out of the kitchen window. "Would you like to slit Nancy O'Connell's fat throat? Yes!" She smiled as she watched two blue jays fight it out over one stray sunflower seed. One of them flew off toward the empty house next door.

"I know!" she finally said. "You haven't watered Jerry's plants in a week. That's something really, really important, Patsy Tazewell. Oh, you are so useful!"

She went to the garage for a watering can and took the keys to Jerry's house from the hook behind the door. As she crossed the road, she looked up at the Fauraults' house. None of them had been at the funeral. Tom's car was gone. The baby was crying, as usual. Maybe Chloe was sick, too. After she finished at Jerry's house, she would stop at Chloe's. And what was really going on at Dolly's house? Three wild ones? Wild how? Dolly had never asked Pat inside. Hmmm.

The thick, sturdy Yanowitz door opened heavily. As she stepped inside, she checked the stained glass. The late sunlight coming through the chunks of dalle de verre cast streaks of color across the hardwood floor. "You were right, Tiffany dear," Pat said. "At least about the door. It could compete with the pearly gates."

The rubber plant in the living room looked almost as sad as Pat felt. "Oh, Jerry," she whispered, "we need you, you deserter." But the noise she heard was not her whispering. There seemed to be a rustling, a swishy, hurrying noise like someone had been sitting on the couch in the living room and had fled to the back of the house. Had someone broken in? Had those boys trashed Jerry's house like they did her backyard?

Setting the watering can on the floor, Pat tiptoed into the dining room. There was nothing there except furniture and two drooping calla lilies. The kitchen was clean, if a little dusty, but there was that noise again. Wind? No—the air was still. Was there someone watching her, keeping an eye on her? Haunting her?

"Don't be ridiculous," Pat said aloud. She went on into what had been Jerry's study, and there she saw it. Another—or the same— bat. "Hey, you," she said. "If you think you're going to become the neighborhood pet, you are sadly mistaken. We prefer cats and dogs. No, not cats," she giggled. "Dogs." As she ducked and cringed, the bat flew past her and down the hall, back into the living room where it had apparently started. And as easily as that, and in spite of the bright light, the bat found fresh air and flew on out the open front door.

She went back to pick up the watering can, taking it to the kitchen to fill it. As she went from plant to plant, she talked to Jerry. "Funny, funny, funny," she said. "Always the joker. So you've changed yourself into a bat. Bully for you, bat man." She went on and on. "I just hope you're happy out there in Stream Whatever. I just hope you've found some lonely and filthy rich old widow to heckle and get batty about." She laughed again. "Aha!" she said. "You ain't got your good wine, Buster. I got it, don't I!" She went to the front of the house and set her can on the porch ready to take home. "Now where is that cellar you were always telling me about?" Back inside, she found the basement stairs, and sure enough, there was a door under the stairs, a door with a lock up where no one would expect it. She pulled Jerry's keys out of her pocket, and sure enough, the third key she tried opened the closet. And sure enough, there were dozens of bottles of Jerry's great wine. How many could she carry? Just two this time. She pulled out a pair, set them on the floor, bolted the door, and took the bottles up the steps.

She couldn't stop at Chloe's house with two bottles of wine and a watering can, so she locked up and went back home. Through the garage. Into the house. "Don't worry," she said, still speaking aloud. "I am not going to drink this now, old chum. Not on top of Scotch and not by myself and not this long before bedtime. First I got to get some brownies out of the freezer and take them to Chloe. Me thinks she is in need of a friend, old chum."

But there were no more brownies in the freezer, and as she headed upstairs to change out of her funeral clothes, the phone rang again. "For heaven's sake!" Pat said. She waited for the second ring and looked at the caller ID. Not a telemarketer. Not Jerry. A 304 number—not a Logan number but definitely West Virginia. Then she remembered. It was the Double-D B&B number. She picked up the receiver and with it in hand started up the stairs.

"I had to tell you, Mrs. Tazewell," Jessie said. "That man called again."

"What man?" Pat asked.

"That Billy John Yeager from North Carolina."

"What did he want?"

"Your address and phone number. I didn't give them to him."

"Good. Who is he anyway?"

"I'm not sure, but he knows a whole lot about you. He said he was looking for his sister, who lived here when they were kids. She and her mother owned this business, and he said his father's name was Yokum but he died when the kids were little."

Pat's hands were shaking. Billy John. Maybe. "Maybe," Pat said, "this guy just talked to my real brother sometime and is now trying to say he is my real brother."

"That's why I didn't tell him where you live and everything."

"Don't." Pat thought a moment. "Did he say anything about having a brother?"

"Just a minute. I wrote everything down, just in case. He said he had a brother who moved to North Carolina when he did, and the brother got married and had three children but was killed when he was driving a race car at the track in Bristol."

"What was his brother's name?"

"He didn't mention a first name. Just said he changed his last name to Yeager, too."

"What should I do?" Pat asked herself, out loud.

Jessie paused. "Well, I guess that's up to you. I'll tell him what he wants to know if you want me to, or I could get his phone number and let you call him if and when you decide to. It's up to you. I promise, I won't do a thing you don't want me to."

"I think you should just tell him to forget it, that you don't know my whereabouts at the moment, which will be true, or whether you ever actually met his sister. I would appreciate that."

That ended the conversation. It also ended Pat's interest in going to see Chloe, brownies or no brownies. Enough is enough, Pat told herself.

But what was she supposed to do with the rest of the dying day? Several things were inevitable: She would worry about Celia, but she would not sit here waiting for the phone to ring. She would think about Frank and wonder what he would be facing in Pittsburgh. She would worry about Roswell and Rosella, but they were out of her hands.

She would think about Colin—he was a part of her that would never disappear.

She would think about Jerry, but what future was there in that? What else was there to think? What, indeed, was there to think about?

Yes, of course. She would pray for world peace and Stephanie and Jack and Priscilla and all of the hungry people in the world and all of the homeless and the sick and the dying and she should be calling the hospice office to see if there was anyone who could use a volunteer.

It was too late now, but, yes, she would do that first thing in the morning. Yes, hospice.

She would keep looking for whoever this woman was who was inhabiting her skin, and she might or might not write more stories that Frank might or might not ever see and that might or might not help her to find this woman who was inhabiting her skin.

Changed into leggings and a Cincinnati Reds t-shirt, Pat couldn't think of a thing she wanted to do but sit down and feel sorry for herself, and she was not about to do that. Pocketbook. Keys. Garage. Car. She started the engine and snapped on her seat belt, and the last of the red lights on the dashboard went out. Plenty of gas, wonder of wonders, thank you, Celia or Walker or whoever. She backed out and, glancing over at Stephanie's house and, seeing nothing out of line, nothing she could possibly help with, she headed out to the highway. West Virginia Public Radio—oh, Lord, another fund drive. She pressed the scan button and found a country music station. Boy or girl owns dog or horse. Boy meets girl or vice versa. Boy and girl fall in love. Boy or girl leaves. Dog or horse dies. Boy or girl comes back to offer condolences. Boy or girl or both ride off on a Harley into the sunset.

What she really needed was some exercise. She took the first exit and headed back toward the housing development, past the golf course, past the day-care center, past the grocery store, and into the parking lot of the spa. Yes! It was open.

She had the exercise room to herself. While she watched CNN on the overhead TV, she put in a good, hard hour on the elliptical trainer. That was enough.

Back in the car, sweating and stimulated, she didn't even think about where she was going next. Her car headed like it was on automatic pilot right toward P.J.'s. Jamie's car was not there, of course, but about fifteen others were, even this early on a week night. Pat pulled into a parking spot, pressed the brake pedal, shifted into Park, and looked up at the building. Had it happened overnight? The boards were gone from the windows and the door. Evergreen shrubs had replaced the flowering plants. Trees had been trimmed. The rich brown letters of "P. J.'s Seasonings" had disappeared, and in their place was a flashing neon sign that alternated from magenta to fuchsia saying, in script, "PLAYTIME, PLAYTIME, PLAYTIME." Two young couples in black leather got out of an old Mustang and, laughing, headed toward the front door. They were followed by a well-dressed, elderly couple who had arrived in a brand new Crossfire. As Pat stared, a new song began on the radio, not Kathy Mattea and not Reba McIntire but some other female singing, "I bet my life on our love. I staked all I had on having you around."

Pat tipped her head back and laughed out loud. "Oh, yes, Mr. Porter Jamison," she said, "oh, yes." Then, looking straight at the building, Pat added, "Screw you, Porter Jamison." She shifted gears again and drove away.

She drove and drove and drove, up into some hills she had never seen before, past huge country estates with horses grazing on thickly grassed fields, past a brand new, red brick elementary school, on up into a rocky, barren area of deserted, has-been cabins that had probably once housed families of eight or ten, past open meadows and along narrow, unlined roads that twisted like black snakes and rolled like sea dragons. In the late daylight, the hills on the other side of the long valley had offered every shade of green, but now they were tinged with purple, and a haze was developing.

She pulled off beside the river and got out, taking off her shoes and wading cold-footed until she found the most beautiful stone she had ever seen. Specks of silver shone in the last of the sunlight. Dipping it back into the river to keep it wet a little longer, Pat staggered back to shore. She picked up her sneakers and put the rock into one of them. She would design this wonderful piece into the stained glass and put it into the river bank in the baptism window. She bent and picked up half a dozen other rocks that looked promising. Then she returned to the car. Putting her stone-filled sneakers on the floor and switching on her headlights, she headed barefoot for home.

Drat! she thought as she came through from the garage and into the kitchen for something—anything—to eat. Three more phone messages on the answering machine, and the phone was even now ringing insistently. Maybe it was Celia!

It was. "We're in Nashville, Mama, and it's a blast, and we met Dolly Parton in person, and we got married, and we are happy, happy, happy!"

Pat froze. "Do you have your medicine?" she managed to ask.

"Enough for a couple more days," Celia said. "That's one reason I'm calling, Mama. Would you pretty, pretty please mail me another batch of each of them? The Radisson in Nashville?"

"Of course," Pat said, relief seeping back into her blood stream. "You're sure you're okay, honey?" she asked.

"Peachy, Mama. Just peachy. You will absolutely love the wedding dress Walker bought for me. It's very swishy, like I could wear it to church."

This was too good to be true. "When will you be back?" Pat asked.

"Soon, Mama. I miss you. Do you know what I dreamed about last night, Mama?"

"Tell me," Pat suggested.

"How Daddy always saved something from his lunch bucket to give to us kids when he came home from the mine. There he was in my dream with Milk Duds and licorice sticks, just like when we were kids, and you know what?"

"What?" Pat asked.

"Walker went out while I was in the shower this morning and found me some Milk Duds. He is so great, Mama!"

Pat smiled.

"And I dreamed," Celia said, "about me being out in the field with Daddy and how he taught me to throw a ball, and in my dream I had Milk Duds in one hand and the baseball in the other." She laughed over the phone. "I can throw a ball better than Walker can, Mama."

"Have a good time, sweetheart. I love you; and I am delighted, thrilled, ecstatic about the wedding. Congratulations, my love, to both of you," Pat said, knowing that she would never, ever tell Celia that she, Pat, had always put the extra candy or crackers in Colin's lunch for him to give to his children and that Colin had also taught her, Pat, to throw a ball.

She called Dolly with the news, and then she was ready for her studio. First, though, the three messages. The first one was a telemarketer. She fast-forwarded through the foreign-sounding voice.

Then Jerry. "Hey, lady," his message said. "I am missing you, and I am finished the park I was building, and they have paid me big money and I am paying for my pal Patsy to come to see her pal Jerry. Call me what day you can come, pal Patsy."

Well, Pat thought.

The third call was from Frank. He was back in Pittsburgh, he said, and he was calling from a pay phone at the gas station, he said, and Nancy had bought herself a gun, he said, and was threatening suicide if he divorced her, and everyone knows that suicide threats must be taken seriously, and that meant, he said, he would have to wait a while before making any further divorce moves, but he would call Pat again tonight, he said, and he would probably go back to Belize until Nancy cooled down and of course he would love it if Pat would go with him. In the meantime, he said, she should remember that he loved her very, very much and that he would—

A huge hole had appeared in Pat's middle. She did not want to hear the rest. She pressed the skip and delete buttons, and the messages were gone.

Still barefoot, she walked to the living room and sat down on the couch. Hands shaking, she picked up the photograph from the side table and said, "You bastard, Colin. What a mess you left me with. If you were still here, you would know. You would probably tell me to be happy for Celia and to let her go and to thank God for Walker and to kiss off—okay, turn loose—our two prodigals with those ridiculous names.

"Second, if you were here, my pal Jerry would not be inviting me to come to Colorado by myself. You and I would both be going, and you would like Jerry a lot, and we would all go rafting down the what's-its-name river and to rodeos.

"Third, old Fonzie O'Connell would be delighted to have you back in his life and I would be the shadow following you two around like back in dear old Durbin.

"Nancy? Well, not even you would know what to do about Nancy. Let's see, is that number three? What about number four?

"Of course. You would tell me to write to our grandson. Call him. Get in touch with Sty somehow. He has a perfectly good grandmother on his mother's side.

"Yes, my beloved Colin, you would even now be over at the Morrisons', and you would have knocked those Faurault terrorists into next week, and they would never have molested Celia and me to begin with. And you would know what's going on at Dolly's. And you would know what I should do about that Billy John Whoever-He-Is."

She sighed. "Oh, Colin—." She set the picture back on the table. "I know. I know. You are gone, and so is that woman you were married to. That Patsy Yokum who became Patsy Yokum Tazewell. There is somebody new living inside her skin, which is aging all too rapidly. Nobody even calls her Patsy anymore. Oh, Jerry."

She stood. "Yes!" she said finally. "Ghosts abound in this house, Colin Tazewell, but I can handle any damned ghost that flits through my door, including those in the form of filthy bats." She took a deep breath. Two deep breaths. "This new woman has decided to take over. This woman is going to move on, move, move, move. This woman has been falling through a trapdoor into emptiness where all of her dreams used to be but where there is now nothing but a big, black hole with a swamp at the bottom." She lifted both arms over her head and clasped them in a stretch. "No more! My feet have been stuck in the muck." She smiled at the photograph. "No more, Mr. Colin Incredible Tazewell. No more!"

Her eyes stung suddenly, and Pat bit her lip, hard. "Oh, shit!" She jumped up and stomped her way to the garage to retrieve her sneakers and the rocks. First something to eat—one does have to eat. Then a long, hot shower. Then, Pat decided, it was time to work on Colin's church window, and after that—Jerry's wine! Maybe a call to invite Dolly to join her.

Food. Shower. Then, in the tiny studio bathroom, she ran water into a faceted blue glass bowl she had made in one of her long-ago Logan classes. She gently placed the river rocks in the water and set them to sparkle under the gooseneck lamp on her desk. As she picked up a pair of trimming scissors, she looked across the road. Her eyes moved to Stephanie's house. Lights were on, and in the clear front window of the Morrisons' living room, Pat could see a stained glass medallion, Tracy headed for heaven.

Turning back to her work table, Pat picked up the sheet of thick paper and began cutting out a piece of the church window pattern. Tomorrow a trip to Paden City for new glass. She glanced out the window once more, this time up into the darkening sky. "Look out, Almighty Creator," she whispered. "Patsy—Patricia Tazewell—is on the move. I'd appreciate it if you would keep your eye on this old stained glass woman."